NO SUCH THING AS
A FREE LUNCH

NO SUCH THING AS A FREE LUNCH

fiction by the same author

A Day to Remember to Forget (1971)
A Virtual Image (1971)
Into Egypt (1973)
No Such Thing as a Free Lunch (1975)
A Superstitious Age (1977)
The Coelacanth (1979)
The Woman in the Tower (1982)
Sense and Sensuality (1985)
Crossing the Water (1986)
The Circus at the End of the World (1998)
Seas Outside the Reef (2000)
Between Man and Woman Keys (2002)
The House in Morocco (2003)
Windstorm and Flood (2007)
Becoming George Sand (2009)
The Third Swimmer (2016)
Paris Still Life (2018)
The Lost Love Letters of Henri Fournier (2018)
Without Her (2019)
Elena, Leo, Rose (2022)
Light over Islands (2024)
Bone Whispers (2024)

NO SUCH THING AS A FREE LUNCH

by

ROSALIND BRACKENBURY

illustrated by

MICHAEL BRACKENBURY

introduced by

A. L. KENNEDY

SANDNESS
MICHAEL WALMER
2025

No Such Thing as a Free Lunch first published 1975
Text © Rosalind Brackenbury 1975
Illustrations © Michael Brackenbury 1975

Introduction first published in this edition
© A. L. Kennedy 2025

This edition published 2025 by

Michael Walmer
Little Pradies
13a Melby
Sandness
Shetland, ZE2 9PL

ISBN 978-1-7635656-7-8 paperback

The publisher gratefully acknowledges the assistance of Robert Heatley and Toby Mercer
in the typesetting and production process for this volume

INTRODUCTION

In a way, a reissue of *No Such Thing as a Free Lunch* is entirely apposite. The booklet appeared in 1975. In the UK economic disparity between rich and poor was hovering around its lowest point in our history. And here we may pause to consider the 70s as a culturally vibrant decade for Britain — not just when it came to music, fashion, film and visual art — and reaching out to Europe. This was a decade of easy booklet publications, underground editions and a diverse publishing landscape stretching from indy magazines to established literary houses making their way, if not making millions. The UK was no longer an empire power but was a significant world player when it came to culture — where once it sent gunboats and troops, it now sent ballet dancers, writers and Shakespearean players — along with bankers, trade envoys and the occasional mercenary. We may never see such relatively sunny days again — certainly not in my lifetime. The daring Rosalind Brackenbury shows here, the embrace of a wider world, the frank but strangely innocent sensuality, the unaggressive Englishness — they are perhaps artefacts from a Britain we decided not to keep. In 21st century Britain, might Brackenbury even have been published, would she have been a sufficiently commercial proposition, sufficiently female in a media-friendly way, sufficiently patriotic to succeed?

If you are old enough to actually recall the 1970s, the energetic artwork scattered through this volume and the outbreak of a wild retro font will seem charmingly familiar. The stories themselves are as deeply and fundamentally of their time as all real art is — and as equally and unmistakably applicable to any time period. From the first paragraph to the lush portrait of the author, I recalled where I had once been. Something about the complexity of rhythms here, the specific sensory palette of word choices returned me immediately to my early childhood in a semi-bohemian university household. Although children don't feature heavily among the stories, Brackenbury's light, yet visceral renderings of adult complications and ambitions, worries, loves and hates returned me to my parents and their friends, to a time of power cuts, impoverished food choices, social and philosophical instability. And there on the horizon was that Other Shore — not too Far Away, but definitely Away: the food of France, the romance of France, the succulently complex language of France, just the *idea* of France. So many characters here seem to dream of sitting outside estaminets reading poems, or looking at the Mediterranean, doing nothing, roaming further, being softly intoxicated, turning into happy people with bright clothes.

This seems particularly plaintive now, as those with control over Britian and particularly England have determined that the UK must wall itself off from the world. Food seethes resentfully in broken supply chains, delicacies disappear or become as unattainably expensive as I remember they were when I was a girl, business with Europe, living in Europe, simply visiting Europe grows ever more difficult. And that old, vaguely undignified, longing for flavour that once haunted my mother is returning. I am forced to recall Brecht's "From a German War Primer":

Among the highly placed

It is considered low to talk about food

The fact is: they have

Already eaten.

The lowly must leave this earth

Without having tasted

Any good meat.

But we are not at war, not in the conventional sense.

Brackenbury is the opposite of disengagement, parsimony. She sweeps into the reader's mind and begins changing things, making things taste better, very much in the manner of the dazzling visitor called Lyndall who appears in one story. Lyndall upends the gently decomposing marriage of Jane and Alex, shows them the possibility of expanding their ambition. Almost as soon as she has become a feature, Lyndall sweeps away again — like a short story. We are told "Jane said, what are we going to do? She meant, having to live without Lyndall. Be different, said Alex; that's all." Quick, deft, remarkable — and we are left in a place where change is neither impossible, nor simply a threat. That's a fine place to live. It is entirely unsurprising that Brackenbury has filled the intervening decades with more books, more writing, more teaching, that she spends her time between a sun-filled house in the US and work with developing writers in Spain.

Brackenbury's prose and imagination are generous. They constantly beckon — *come and see, come and taste, come and say, come and feel, come and be*. The sheer livingness of life is everywhere — in plants, objects, landscapes and animals, in the wild futures people run towards, or amputate before they become too overwhelming. Food and drink are everywhere, challenging the bleak days of Blue Nun and Angel Delight, instant coffee and grey cabbage — here are olives eaten near their trees, good wine and good dope, here there are even plain suburban folks maddened by their need to gorge on seafood, on salt, before they plunge back into an undersea life with gills, far, far away from Baked Alaska and mediocrity. Couples are delighted by mouthfuls described with deft, unpretentious accuracy, they snack together and treat each other to fine dining and taste, taste, taste. Individuals enjoy proper coffee and unfamiliar meals in new places with France the reliable, delicious destination, perhaps attained with the help of a travel agency that 'smells of foreign money' — how entirely perfect. This is reading as intoxication and it's a joy.

One would be able to guess that Brackenbury is a poet simply from her intense accuracy, her beautiful little word parcels of dense meaning. In this she resembles Muriel Spark and Raymond Carver, but with added Technicolour and an excellent *carte du jour*.

Dans le train arrives late in the collection but, as it flirts its way between fiction and autobiography, it cuts deep into the author's vision of writing. "Fiction" it declares "is an assault in the night". Although the narrative does deal with a violent, if peripheral, drunk these stories are not themselves an unpleasant assault, more the kind of contact one might expect from a warm wave in the shallows, being greeted by a large, friendly dog, or an enthusiastic lover. The one story which comes, appropriately, closest to shock focusses on a young girl during the single day on which she first sees sex — an adult couple briefly glimpsed in copulation — and then death, when she goes to a friend's house and finds their elderly relative dead. The inarticulate feeling of someone confronted by so much strangeness is wonderfully conjured.

Brackenbury is cerebral and unsettling in the manner of Spark. Children are disturbed by their parents; parents are baffled by their children. In *Horsemen* a baby's screams are 'like a rasp on metal' and her parents know 'that the baby was stronger than they, that she would not give up'. But she lacks Spark's sharpened morality and Edinburgh stiffness. Only Brackenbury could turn a staid little village tradition into a wild communal dance and then an act of revolution, repossessing land, when the squire's dominance 'has all gone on for too long.'

Like Carver's couples and individuals, the characters in these stories are adrift in lives they don't understand, in ill-fitting relationships. Often the intervention of a stranger is what brings light. Certainly, there is more sunshine here than Carver tends to find. Even in *The World's End* — a story about the literal end of the world — there is passionate gentleness. Taking her cue from both the apocalypse and the point at which London's hip Kings Road was generally agreed to lose its vibe,

Brackenbury chronicles a very orderly, very English end of everything, Suburban people make the best of it, under the extremely ill-defined threat of imminent global extinction. Eventually, a young mother sits isolated, cradling her youngest child, wondering when to give out the poison kindly provided to avoid the vague horrors ahead — and wondering when to kill herself. She is interrupted by an old man who persuades her not to murder herself out of unknown fear. He tells her that he knows she is thinking '(t)hat all this beauty, this subtlety, this complexity of evolution, that it is all ending, just like that.' He persuades her to live right up to the end, to see it, to be curious and human and alive. And, as it turns out, the world doesn't end — it is only very changed, and she and her children and the kind stranger walk forward into it, starting again in the reward for their fearlessness.

Brackenbury understands the light that prose can give in dismal times, she writes of the comfort in having a hand to hold in the dark. This little collection is a light to follow and hand to hold. I'm so glad it's back in circulation, here for all of us.

A. L. KENNEDY
Banffshire, November 2024

Contents

No Such Thing as a Free Lunch

The day, the place, the hour, were of a greenness neither could have imagined; green leaves in the greenest of months, May, in the south where green flourishes into its summer brilliance in such a matter of minutes; green depth of shadow, dappled green, salad green where the light fell; and green napkins now, green tablecloth, a mixed bowl of green lettuce and chopped darker chives set before them. He thought it was like lunching under water; like swimming towards each other through clear depths, among weed; as if the afternoon, later, were a bright surface to be reached. Both of them would come up sated, limp; to a drier atmosphere where the light burned and flies touched them and heat and effort began again. He drank another glass of rosé; and it was as if his head were blown empty and his brain floated loose above it. Vaguely he was aware that there would be a bill; but the waiters were discreet, lulling the diners through the two long hours of lunch, hovering not too near, respecting confidences, leaving the two of them, the lovers in their foreign clothes, to the last. William went out between courses to buy cigarettes, the taste of veal in his mouth that had long been unaccustomed to meat. It was like having one's own blood on the palate, as after sucking a cut dry. His thick-soled sandals struck the pavement; clack-clack, the sharp echo of midday in the sun. The back of his neck burned. He moved slowly, a pulse marking time. Between the cars and the trees and the people of this city, between all the unknown things and then back to her; to that known face, expectant look, slight smile, vagueness, elbows upon the table among the glasses and bowls. Down, down steps, cut by the sudden cool; as into a pool, an aquarium. Swimming between the other tables, the subdued constant voices of others, the diners, the couples, the parallel eaters of lunch; hot, large, in dusty clothes he came; scattering ripples. She raised her glass to him, drank the remains of the wine, a blur in her eyes. They had come too quickly in from sun and strenuous exercise, drunk too quickly, filling empty stomachs with the chill and biting wine. He saw now that she was in love with the calm, the quiet here, the expensive quiet. With couples who murmured to each other, forks raised, polished heads delicately forwards like tame birds; with middle-aged women, beautifully dressed, pastel, exchanging gossip over sole meunière; with a finely sewn seam, a glossy fall of hair, with cloth, with heavy china, with cooled wine falling into glass. Soothed, calmed by smooth surfaces. She said nothing to him, but he saw it in her gaze about her, as if at last she was perfectly happy. She looked past him, and he knew that here he did not fit; whereas she, she felt herself at ease here, she was the missing piece of the jigsaw, the small corner of the photograph that had not quite been made distinct. She emerged from darkness and shadow as the sun moved just slightly, glinting down between the white metal tables, edging the shaggy umbrellas that moved like giant wigs in the breeze. She became clear. She belonged. Her white arms folded upon the tablecloth only slightly reddened from the rude sun that morning; her hair falling in the clear dark outline of a bell; her eyes green, green as the table linen, matching, as if there had not been enough different colour to go round. She smiled at him, then, and asked for a cigarette.

They had been, that morning, in a field where poppies blew open, red among green standing corn. At the edge, rather, at the prickly edge of that field, beneath little oak trees that were lately unfolding their soft leaves. Soft, gentle the landscape looked, until you lay down in it. He remembered the marks upon her back, from twigs and earth. But the corn was a cover, from the hot and open sky. Laying her down, laying her out; carefully, he remembered, with a qualm for her white indoor skin upon that hardness; and himself, his back joyfully arched to the heat, buttocks, shoulder blades burning as he moved, like a worker, a labouring creature, like a weapon to that earth. She lay and looked beyond him; the loose silk petal of a poppy detached itself and floated upon her throat; she was sacrificial, silent. He sat up naked, a big dark man tanned brown beneath sparse straight hair, always that colour, even in winter; his own skin hardly feeling the scratchiness of grass that she complained of. She did it for him. Pretended to enjoy making love out of doors. Would have preferred a bed, sheets, the cool of a room behind shutters, the comforting cold cleanliness of tiles. Remorseful, he had suggested the restaurant. She had sat up, then, and begun to brush her fine coppery hair, stroking it out before the wind. Her white shirt still open to the waist, as she had carelessly put it on against the sun, but hardly crumpled, not stained; as if she had unconsciously dressed, that morning, for a restaurant in town. Her skirt blown like a large patterned spider's web against a bush. She said, aren't you going to put some clothes on? Did not like, perhaps, seeing him sitting about like that. He stood up and brushed the burrs and grasses from the insides of his thighs, and looked out absently across the countryside, buttoning his trousers. (And now, as the waiter brought back that large decorated menu, and they looked, to choose what dessert they would have, he felt it all still, the dried stiff patches on the insides of his legs, the prickles still there, ants perhaps; did she, looking so coolly outside herself, feel the same?) There had been nightingales, calling and calling to each other in the oak woods; the long questing whistle and then the chuckling song; like an echo, a suggestion of the sexual act. They were everywhere, they seemed to move all a-round them, like an audience. When they shouted out at last, the nightingales followed. And he heard them again, a little further away, as he stood, slowly dressing himself again, watching swallows dive about the cornfield, looking out towards far distant mountains; losing himself for a moment in a blueness of distance that was like contemplating the rest of his own life. He was quiet, it was a quiet moment. And she sat still, waiting for him, her hands joined around her knees beneath the long cotton skirt, her hair falling into two parts about her bent white neck. Separate and yet at ease in their quite different thoughts and feelings; always apart and yet at times like this in harmony. He thought, if one could live like this; feeling and accepting differences, letting this silence work; in this landscape, in such beauty. It seemed that for the first time he was perhaps looking at the rest of his life, at years he had not yet discovered, never before contemplated. Far mountains, edging the sky. How could one, after this, live out of their sight?

It was then that they had seen the lizard. He came out from beneath the grey stone upon which William had left his shirt, and he was green, green like the rest of that day, green and patterned as a fresh courgette, polished and bright. He put out his head first and looked at them, black eyes opaque. He was motionless for a long moment. William caught Alice's hand, fascinated, holding her back so that she might see. Together they stared at the lizard and the lizard stared back at them. The corn rustling was the only movement. Overhead the sky was poised; blue, empty. In this silence the creature came out, licking his sharp black tongue out, nosing forward his blunt head. His tail, following him out of the dark hole, incredibly long, tapering. His feet just paler than the rest of him, a clear jade green. He was a luxury object, brilliant, cool, jewelled amid the roughness of grass and scrub. And Alice wanted to hold him and keep him, to take him with her, keep that beauty hers; she spoke, even softly, and he was gone. Back into the invisible hole, faster than light moves, it seemed; before they could blink. Gone. William said, lizards are very wise creatures, he could feel that we were here, all along. He must have been old, don't you think, to have been so large? What a beauty. And he, picking up his sandals, was ready now to move on, saw that it was time to go; whereas Alice stood staring at the place where the lizard had gone, rooted in some deep disappointment. Come on, Alice in Wonderland, he teased her, I thought you were longing for your lunch?

Two great mounds of chantilly cream emerged from silver cups, were set before them, freckled with grated chocolate; frost upon the silver as if it were winter. The cold shuddered between one's teeth, the touch of the spoon set one all on edge. Heat and chill, sunlight and shadow; artfully copied in the preparation of food. He felt as if he were being played with, being tossed to and fro, into the laps of opposing sensations, opposing worlds. And Alice calmly spooned hers up without a frisson. And across the little passageway between tables, the two women of a certain age, meeting perhaps after a morning at the hairdressers and before an afternoon shopping in town, were eating exactly the same thing. A party at the table behind them ordered chilled melon and began to argue among themselves about wine, the waiter standing patiently like a nurse at a bedside, pencil tapping only slightly. One of the women in the party, very dark in a pink turban, spread out her brown fingers to admire the exactness of their scarlet tips. A little dog, tied by the lead to a table leg, snuffed at a few green fallen chestnut leaves and was given a bowl of spaghetti dotted with cubes of meat. Around them all, as the breeze lifted the spread leaves of the tree, chestnut blossom fell in pink and white gusts, into wine glasses, into coiled mounds of hair, onto clean, ironed cloth and into the clefts of spiral napkins. The solitary man in the dark suit at the far table pressed a napkin to his lips and ordered coffee. The waiters moved more slowly, carrying away the piles of heavy plates. It was all nearly at an end, it would have to finish; with just the wind in the leaves and the empty, ruined tables, and the piles of washing up to be done indoors; and the dim roar of traffic outside, beyond this island. What would they do? After this, how step back into the ordinary world? He and Alice, to go to the bank, buy cartons of milk and washing powder, provisions to carry back to the camp he had thought was home? He saw in the droop of her lips, her regret, that the pleasure ended. Anything he could suggest — a church, a walk, a museum — anything they could afford, would not do; would not be enough. She existed here; in a fin-de-siècle cushioned luxury that he could not afford, that was not his to offer. She lived in a different time, a different world; her fingers too spread long and tapered, the nails pale moons, the wrists fragile as a greyhound's bones. And the conviction that had come to him that morning, the vision of their future life, faded and began to disappear. A cottage, he had thought, ruined even, a place that would be theirs to construct and repair; good earth, vegetables, the pleasure of digging and planting, sweat all over one from hard work in the heat of the day. The simple production of all that they needed, so that they would not long for anything from outside. He could do it, he knew; his strong hands instinctively grasped the task at hand; he could build and carpenter and dig ditches and cut wood, he could fence his little world and make it work for him. A goat, he had thought, so that they could have milk and make cheeses. Chickens, too, and a couple of ducks, geese to keep down grass and weeds. For him, it would be enough; realising it, he had suddenly known himself at that moment, recognised who he was. He had not talked about it to her, not yet. The evening would have been time enough, when they were sitting outside their little tent, drinking their rough red wine from the bottle, eating a sandwich perhaps, watching the sun go down. Now he saw it; that one could leave things too late. There was a chance; and one looked away, moved, missed the moment; and it was gone. He thought now of a small stone house in the middle of England, so far from here, under that perpetual greyness of low sky; where he could work, where he could live. All at once he was eager to go home, to bring this holiday, this last fling, this absurd spending of time and money, to its end. They drank their coffee, talking about the other people in the restaurant, the ones who had just left; who had left dirty plates and napkins and cups stained with lipstick, yet who had paid and gone.

Alice said, those two women, was it their husbands or their lovers that they were talking about, do you think? And, funny how interesting other people's lives are, even the pills they take and the diseases they think they've got. She was scornful, ironic; yet not of the lives these women led, but of their age, that encouraged this self-solicitude. She was fascinated by them, he saw it. She had noticed the rings that they had, heavy upon white fingers, and the clothes, the scarfs signed by Ted Lapidus, the coats flung to one side with the Daniel Hechter label inside; and the shrewd witty way their mouths had pursed, the world of sensual complicated pleasure they evidently shared, massages and sauna baths and hair appointments and lovers. They had lovers, these old women. He said, oh, surely not, they were probably just talking about their sons. But Alice knew, it was as if she had written the script; she told him now exactly what had been said. Suddenly he was angry, as if a long slowburning fuse in him were at its inflammable end. He pointed to the only man left in the restaurant, the business man with the smooth cap of black hair who wore his dark suit as if he had been born in it, who was finishing his meal with a cognac now.

You could have him, William said to her. He would buy it all for you. He still has enough millions of francs left to go on living like this. He'd keep you in lunches and silk dresses and soft leather boots. For as long as anything like this exists, for as long as it's true, this dream, this fantasy, for as long as it seems to work. As long as anybody has it, he'll have it. Le fric, as they say — and he the angry Englishman rubbed his two fingers together in that vulgar gesture; protesting against the freedom of the female to pick, choose, alight where she wants to, to choose a hunting ground, to join with the rich and strong; burning himself up now with envy and anger and French wine. Alice looked at him with her slow green gaze. He saw that she was surprised, that she did not understand. She had enjoyed her lunch, in the way she enjoyed all that was natural to her, and she was simply surprised.

What do you mean? she said. What are you talking about? He gestured, his empty hands taking in the little garden of the restaurant that was set back so tidily from the traffic, the passing crowds, the constant noise of the city, from the few North African beggars that he had seen on his way to buy cigarettes. He said, all this; that's all. In his pocket he had about sixty francs, and he was afraid that it would not be enough to pay for what they had eaten.

What? All what?

It just scares me a bit.

What does? She made a little shrug with her hands; baffled, even amused.

There won't be any more of it, he said. It's just a dream. At once he wondered if the world outside ever mirrored anybody's dream; of

13

peace, of self-sufficiency. Never mind, he said; if you enjoyed it.

Didn't you? I thought it was marvellous. That sauce we had with the veal, it was delicious, I can't imagine what it was made of. Cream, there must have been, and white wine, but what was the herb? Tarragon, do you think?

Tarragon? He looked across the table, across the loose dark patterns of the reflected leaves. Tarragon, perhaps.

Anyway, it was lovely, for a treat. Thank you. Thank you for bringing me. But I don't mind if we don't do it again. If you don't like it. But I mean, if it's here now, why not enjoy it? Even if it is the last time. She looked down, away from him, her last words spoken on a note of resignation. The last man in the restaurant got up to go, leaving a fluttering pile of notes tucked under an empty glass. He was quite young, perhaps five years older than William; good looking in his suit with his crisp shirt and broad tie patterned with small flowers; his face narrow and dark, a Mediterranean face, Greek or Jewish perhaps in origin, his hair cut like smooth cat's fur, growing to a peak. He turned, before leaving, and smiled a little formally or perhaps shyly and wished them a good afternoon. His eyes, William noticed, were black and deep even while he smiled; eyes of an older generation; suddenly like the lizard's, past showing any transient expression. He had looked for an intent moment at Alice, and now he nodded briefly to William, as if they were already acquaintances.

There he goes, said William, as they stood up together at the little white table, to collect matches and cigarettes and bags and books, to leave the right amount of money on the plate; there goes the last of the millionaires.

Poor man, said Alice.

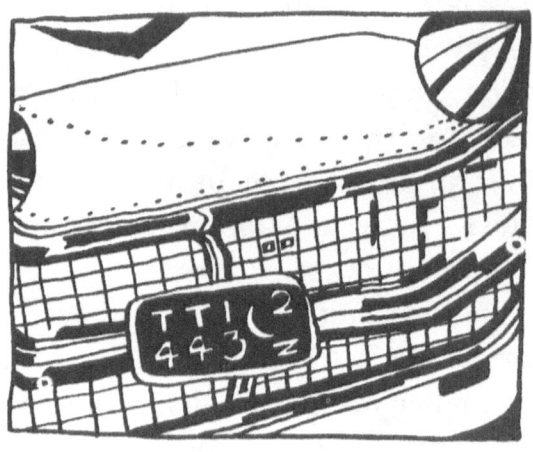

The Visitor

There are times, when a knock comes at the front door, and the door opens; when a person appears, around whom the world, the evening, suddenly reels. You stand quite still, and it is the world that moves.

Well, hi. You don't remember me?

It was then that Jane realised that she had been waiting for somebody; for this knock, this voice coming out of the night; also that there are people in one's life whom one always greets with both relief and fear.

Lyndall. Lyndall Watson. You remember that time in Greece? She remembered a ship sailing between the steep walls of the Corinth Canal; a ship in a street, in a corridor; twilight and their guitars, and chewing chicken legs up in the high bows; another life. She thought, no, I do not want to be reminded. Not now. Not of that freedom. I cannot cope with seeing Lyndall Watson now.

Can I come in? A swing of long hair forward into the light, the upturned furry coat collar, Lyndall's breath on the cold damp air, December, England. And her profile as she turned suddenly to see who it was who stood behind Jane. It was he, Alex, who stepped forward without hesitation, exclaimed with delight, took Lyndall and kissed her on both cheeks, as if they were abroad; as Jane could not have done. Who said all the things, you, here, how amazing, how lovely; all the things one should say. Too late, Jane exclaimed too, and kissed, and welcomed. And Lyndall was coming into the flat, and looking eagerly around her and exclaiming too; while Jane felt her own lack, her bulk, her inability. She was throwing down her worn Afghan coat upon the sofa, dropping her woven bag upon the floor, turning her head to catch at her hair and hold it back with one hand at the nape of her neck in a gesture that was suddenly familiar; graceful, easy, pleased to see them, that was all.

So, you're still together, that's marvellous that's great! As if they were the only unchanged entity in a world that she had seen change around her. Are you married? My, that's really great! And you're having a baby, Jane! When's it due? Aren't you lucky? Aren't you pleased?

And Jane, holding her two arms across the round bulge beneath her smock, had been uselessly trying to hide it, trying to keep it out of Lyndall's bright gaze. In the spring, she said, in April, we think. The pain that she had felt when he moved forward so easily to greet Lyndall was still with her, seemed to grow. She felt all unfitted for the moment, all out of key. She wished that Lyndall would go away now, leave them, not ask. After that first quick, intuitive knowledge of relief — you, at last! After that — now, go. She watched Lyndall go round the little room, their sitting room — you don't mind me looking at your things? — saw her turn from looking at a painting, an ornament, a row of books, with that quick warm smile — I just want to see where you're at, what you're thinking about? She saw that Lyndall's arms coming out from her short sleeved woven shirt were long and brown, and that her neck beneath the twisted golden hair was brown, and her feet bare in espadrilles, her jeans worn and bleached, her small breasts naked beneath the thin white cotton, swinging just slightly as she moved. She was dressed for summer, for hot weather, and here she was in a dank city in the midlands, in a cold dark northern night. Jane wished that Alex could not see the long column of Lyndall's neck and the small dark shapes of her nipples. She said, where have you come from? Meaning, why are you dressed like that? Lyndall smiled, her eyebrows raised and hands stretched out as if to balance herself. Well, that's a pretty long story. But no, where I've just come from, is Turkey. Why Turkey? I'll tell you all that, later. I can stop over for a night, can I? I mean, I don't need a bed, just a corner with some blankets would be fine. Then we can really talk. You must have so much news, look at you, married, having a baby, I'm really longing to hear about it all, so I'll just tell you this much, now. I've just driven from Turkey, there was a guy I had to see in London, and then I thought, well, I still had your old address, so I turned up there, Fulham, wasn't it, and a woman told me you'd moved here. So, here I am.

Here? All the way from Fulham, just in case we were still here? We might have moved to Newcastle, or even Edinburgh, by now.

Well. And she smiled at them. That's no great distance, if you've come from Turkey. And before that I was in North Africa. Morocco, Algeria. That's a great place. D'you know it? D'you know a place called Tamanrasset, in Algeria? Well, I'll tell you all about that, later. Then I got to Turkey, with a mixture of auto-stop and getting on trains, and in Istanbul I met this guy who gave me a car, and it was getting a bit cold, and anyway I wanted to see this other guy in London who I'm in love with; so I thought, hey, here's my chance, I'll go to England. It just took me a few days. And he was out, which was a shame, but you were in. So — and she spread her hands and smiled at them as if she could wish for no better, and spread her legs before her comfortably in a long stretching movement, freeing her feet from the worn espadrilles as she moved.

A car? A man gave you a car? Where is it? Alex was like a detective, leaning forward to listen; his eager dog-face, brown alert eyes; as if he could not make sense of all the evidence.

Outside in the road. Round the corner. I'll go down and get my things in a minute. There's some Turkish wine in the trunk, I'll get that, and we could drink it. My, but it's good to see you both again. How've you *been*? and she caught them both quite suddenly in her arms, embraced them, let them go, laughing, so that they were closer to each other than they had been for some weeks. Then she went downstairs with Alex to get a bag and the bottle out of her car, and Jane made coffee, and went to the cupboard to find blankets, and pulled the camp bed out from under shoes and pillows, and set it up in a corner of the sitting room; and waited for them to return. She heard Alex's step upon the stairs, suddenly springy, and heard a note in his voice that she had missed. The coffee began to percolate, bubbling up faster and faster until it was a continuous gurgle. She set out the heavy green china cups, found cheese and biscuits in the larder; and was suddenly excited herself, preparing a feast, a picnic, suddenly began to sing. A song, a voice, a feeling long forgotten. She was singing when Alex and Lyndall came back into the room.

They sat up late that night, she who had been going to bed so early, feeling so tired, weighed down, exhausted by the extra weight she carried, and he who had to get up for work in the morning, who felt terrible at the office if he did not have his eight hours' sleep. The bottle of Turkish wine emptied, and Alex went to find a bottle of supermarket red in the kitchen. Biscuit crumbs lay everywhere on the floor that Jane had, that morning, so laboriously swept. Lyndall pulled out a packet of marijuana wrapped in thick plastic, given to her by the Turk in Istanbul, and rolled a fat joint; sitting cross-legged, she smoked and smiled and passed it sometimes to Alex. Jane had a taste, filled her mouth, with the sweetish burning smoke, but felt she wanted no more. The evening was enough as it was, no extra clarity was needed. She felt her body strangely throb, as Lyndall talked; as if a drum beat somewhere, as if it were waking her, waking her up; as if from tomorrow everything would be changed. Lyndall talked of North Africa and of the flowering plants in winter and the Arab horses running and the camel trains that pass in the desert; of dawn and travel and trains whose roofs she had lain on, to go a hundred, two hundred miles, and dust and sand storms and drinks made of bitter herbs; of Roman buildings standing in drifts of sand and of white beaches with nobody on them; of an Arab lover in Marrakesh, whose name was Khaled, and of the English lover in Corfu, whose name was Harry, and who lived in North London; of the bodies of men and animals, of movement, of a world in which all was a long dance, a fluid living chain that met no barriers of country or of language, which she carried with her, of which she was a part. Having said that she wanted to hear their news first, she could not hold herself back; it was as if she had arrived here burning with a message, with news of the world outside, and could not help telling it all to them, with this urgency, at once. The clock struck two, three. Jane yawned, in spite of herself, and felt the child inside her move up, clench itself into a hard lump with square edges, like a box inside her. It was at night that it always grew active, kicked at her; usually she lay in bed and stared up at the pale square of the ceiling across which the beams of car lights moved, and heard the noise of traffic outside, even at two, three in the morning, and waited for time to pass. There would be Alex, asleep beside her, a little restless, sometimes putting out a hand for her as he would not have done, waking. For how long had they lived like this, in this limbo of greyness and lack of feeling? Only now did she think of it as this, as a definite period of time in her life; now she saw it. What had they done? How were they? Lyndall wanted to know, yes, but they were both ashamed to tell her. We came back from Greece at the end of the last summer vacation, when Alex had graduated, and we decided to get married and then Alex got a job in the midlands, on the management side, and we moved up here, and Jane taught for a while and then got pregnant; and for a year, two years, longer even, we have lived in this convenient flat on this main road on a bus route into town, near to the shops, near to the relaxation classes, and here we have slowly, gradually stopped speaking to each other, stopped making love, here we have come to speak politely but coolly to each other, without passion, without love or anger. For how long? Just while time passed. They say that it will all be different when the baby is born. Alex is working hard, expecting promotion, a higher salary; then we will put down the deposit on a house and move out, into the suburbs, into the country, so that the baby will have somewhere to play. What else will happen? As little as possible, we hope, to change our plans. Both of them, looking at each other, knew that they were ashamed, did not want to say this, admit such failure. And it was Lyndall only who enthused about their life, their flat, their belongings. I really like that painting, and the rug's great. Did you bring that back from Greece that time? You know, it's got a really good atmosphere, here. Where'll you have the baby, here or in hospital? I've always felt it must be scary for them, being born in a hospital, you know, coming out into all that harsh bright light, and people in uniform and everything. You must make the baby lots of lovely coloured clothes. They look so good in bright, dark colours, and people will dress them in baby blue and pink. It's all wrong. A baby is such a distinct personality, not just a little blob, don't you agree? You know, I really envy you, Jane. I think I'd give up everything, right now, to have a baby growing inside me, a baby from the man I'm in love with. He's beautiful, he'd make such fine children. Only, being alone, moving about so much, it's difficult. It wouldn't be fair right now, I guess. But I think it's the most important thing that can happen to you, having a baby, watching it grow. It's the only real thing in life, after all, sex and love and babies. Don't you find it's the most extraordinary time, now? Don't you feel tremendously excited about it all?

Jane and Alex were, shy, ashamed; and Jane thought that he looked younger than he had, although tired. I tell you what, Lyndall went on, I've just thought. I've got lots of stuff in my bag, cloth, you know, from all over. Morocco and Turkey and Greece, mostly Arab things, I'll show you. We could make some lovely things for you to wear, and for the baby. Have you got a sewing machine? Have you made any clothes yet? These'll look just beautiful, don't you think? And she pulled from her battered little bag yards of woven and embroidered cloth, fine and light as the things she wore; scarlet and dark blue, purple, golden, black and silver; all the colours of camel trains and markets, brilliant birds and flowering trees; and spread them all about her on the floor. I don't want them. What would I do with them? I've got enough things. They're for you, for your baby. We can start making them tomorrow.

In the morning, Jane came into the room to find Lyndall standing at the window, dressed in her jeans and shirt, looking out. The blankets and sheets were all neatly folded on the little bed; as if she had struck camp. She nearly cried out to her, but you aren't going, you can't go yet, we haven't made the clothes! But Lyndall turned and smiled, said, can I give you a hand with breakfast? I'll make the coffee, if you'll show me where all the things are. And Jane saw that she was not going, not yet. Alex came in, a little pale, knotting up his tie to the buttoned collar of his shirt. Lyndall had not seen him dressed for work before, and he felt shy, like this, as if there were some need to apologise. She raised her eyebrows at him and he muttered something: just a disguise; and sat down at table. The women brought him toast and coffee and set the plates around. For the first time in weeks, a pale disc appeared in the sky beyond the roofs seen from the kitchen window; a watery winter sun. The sky was a bright pale grey; the mist might lift, might clear; they might be able to see at last. Jane saw the first gleam upon the inside of the window jamb, the first splash of shadow upon the floor. And something was puzzling her. She could not remember whether or not it were a dream; that sensation she had had, in the night, of a hand moving down over the curve of her naked stomach, pushing up her nightdress, coming to caress her between the legs. She had moved away, closed her legs, in dream or in fact;

even in the depths of sleep guarding the child against the earthquake of orgasm, pushing that possibility away. But the hand had continued to stroke her buttocks, for a moment or two after that. There was no way of knowing, now, if it had been a dream. She looked across at Alex, who was cutting and buttering toast, and saw his glittering eye. He was white, thin, young today; fatigue showing under his eyes. She saw his hands, hairless and straight-fingered. Knew that he wanted Lyndall; for who would not? She herself was so distorted now, and full of fears. She sat back, her stomach pushing up her flowered shirt in that clear round bulge of a first child, and warmed her hands upon her coffee cup. Considered it, this knowledge. Lyndall sitting there sipping her coffee, brown hands upon the table, body fluid and light beneath those thin summer clothes. For the first time, Jane considered without fear the possibility of Alex making love to another woman; thought, if it were Lyndall, I should not mind. Something important would be happening to him; he would be woken up, made aware, made lighter of heart and body; and how could one deny him that? She felt sad, often, when she saw how worn out he became, working, and travelling to and fro, and paying bills and writing letters; when she saw, in the evenings, the long, tired slump of his body; when she realised how he would feel the added weight of being a father. A young man, still, but tied by the foot, packed like a beast of burden. Suddenly, this morning, she wanted to set him free. And outside the pale light of the sun strengthened just perceptibly, as if to strengthen her.

When Alex had gone to catch his bus — a wave to Lyndall, a brief simulated kiss for Jane, grab for his briefcase, flattening stroke to his short red hair, and off — the two women stood side by side at the sink to wash and dry the dishes. Lyndall washed, bending over the little sink; the smooth knobs of her spine showing through her shirt. Jane moved to and fro, hitching herself between the table and the chairs, reaching up to put things away with one hand often automatically laid to the small of her back. They did not talk for a while. Both of them felt the impact of Alex's departure. There was still the dust to settle, the room to quieten, after his going. Jane felt it each morning, the disturbance he left behind him; she was left to cope with it, she felt, with that restlessness of his, and her own long hours of solitude, of waiting, and then the impossible intrusion of his return home, just as she had reached some kind of acceptance of being alone. Now, with Lyndall there, it felt different. She knew that today would have its own possibilities and events and that she and Lyndall would live it together; so that when Alex came home, it would not be an intrusion but an easy meeting, an exchange of the day's experiences. Lyndall began to clear the kitchen table completely and pull her pieces of material about. Have you made any clothes for yourself? You aren't thinking of going on wearing that shirt and trousers, are you, they're getting too tight already. Look, you must have something grand and sexy. It's terribly sexy, being pregnant, you must really feel good. Look, what about this velvet, shall we try that? You show me where the machine is, and I'll get it set up. She organised Jane now, moving her about. Outside, the day grew fine. It was early December; the damp and fog had been around the flat like a cold wrapper, for weeks, making it impossible for Jane to find the energy to go out. But now she pushed up the sash of the kitchen window and leaned out for a moment, remembering how it would be in spring. There would be daffodils down there, and she with her new baby sitting under that one tree in the tiny back garden behind the flat. Lyndall set the machine going, pulled a large pair of scissors out of her bag and began to snip up the velvet. Every now and then she held up a piece against Jane, fitting it to her shoulders or down her arm. No pattern, no proper measurements, Jane thought; watching the inspired and apparently random hacking and pinning together of the material, that fell like mown grass upon the table. Take off your things a minute, Lyndall told her. The cold of the inside of the velvet lay against her skin. The baby kicked and heaved and she grew tense against it. Lyndall said, relax, you're all knotted up. And she shut her eyes and stood there, the light red inside her lids, feeling Lyndall's fingers pin and fit and smooth; feeling the relief of allowing another person to take over a part of her life at last.

By one o'clock, Lyndall had finished the dress, and there were only the seams and hem to sew. It was dark green, with long sleeves and a low neck. Jane stood in it before the long mirror in the hall. Lyndall said, you look beautiful; and Jane saw it, for the moment. She saw herself as the pale central stem of a lords-and-ladies plant, seeing how her neck showed white above the discreet woodland green, and how the bulge where the baby was seemed just right, for the first time. She felt all of a piece, now; as if the tensions and the battles inside no longer existed, or at least, might be resolved. Thank you, she said to Lyndall, who stood there beside her in the mirror, boyish in her old clothes, beside herself, suddenly stately in the dress.

It was a pleasure. I love making things for people. But what about your poor baby, you can't be the only one with something to wear, what are we going to make for him? I tell you what, let's have a drink and something to eat, and then this afternoon we can make him some little things out of this Arab stuff. Okay?

They poured glasses from the remains of the red wine and made sandwiches of pate and cheese, and sat by the window to feel the faint touch of the sun. Lyndall said, I couldn't live without the sun. It's why I travel so much, partly. I couldn't stay, you know, in the north, I couldn't live with a weak little sun like that. I think it must be really hard.

Jane said, curious, do you always know exactly what you need? And then just try and get it? Or do you ever try and do without something and see if you can get over it? I'm just in-terested, that's all.

Do I try and do without things? Well — and Lyndall spread out her fingers, looked down at them as if they held a message, while she thought. I guess I do without ordinary things, you know, regular meals, baths, beds, money, going to the hairdresser, eating candy, having proper clothes, all that kind of thing, but I guess too that's not a real effort, it's gotten easy for me now. Sure, I'm uncomfortable now and then and I miss like hell having a real good soak in a hot tub, having something clean and pretty to put on. But then I think of Main Street, America, and all that entails, and I stop wanting them. But other things, the things I know I need? The sun, movement, travel, good friendships, good orgasms; no, I don't try and pass up those things, because they're my life. I mean, what else have I? I don't see any point in trying to give that up. But one thing strikes me, Jane, is that the less you care about what happens to you, the better life gets. The less you worry, the happier. If you can give it all away, if you see what I mean, you're liable to get it all back, and more. I don't mean, like some sort of pinball game, but just that if you take the risk, you lose everything, then you gain something else. Hell, I'm not being very clear, am I.

Jane said, I think I see. She wanted time, time to take all this in, to see how it applied to her, to find out what it was, this colossal fear at her very root, that hurt so much.

What's the matter, have you got a pain? D'you want to stretch out for a while? Here, you give me that and go lie on the couch. Hell, I've been making you do too much.

No. No. I'm all right. It's just something you said. There's just something that really hurts me at the moment, when this baby goes all hard, like something screwed up tight inside me, and then kicks out, I can't stand it, it's what makes me afraid. And she bent over herself, over the hard bulge, feeling that terrible angularity of the child inside. Lyndall's arm went round her and her hand lay upon her forehead. She felt herself uncurled, laid out, made to relax, It's all linked up, Lyndall was saying, and you're right at the centre of it, now. That's why having a baby must be so great, you give up everything, and you get everything back times a hundred, All that getting big and wondering how it'll ever get out. I wonder that, sometimes, I really do.

Christ almighty, I think, how the hell's a whole person going to get out through my little cunt. But even if it splits you open, you've done it, you've made it, you've given somebody else life. That's just the most incredible thing. Now, are you okay? Shall we start on those clothes? I tell you what, you lie there a moment and see if you can figure out if it's a boy or a girl, and then I'll start cutting up the stuff.

In the evening, friends were coming to dinner. Jane found that she had forgotten them, had wanted to forget. Remembering, thinking of the food she still had to cook, she wanted nobody to come; for there only to be herself and Lyndall. Not even Alex, not even him. Just herself and Lyndall, as they had been all day, in this intimacy of working side by side. But Lyndall said, forestalling her: that'll be fun, I really like cooking, only I never get the chance to do any. What're you having? Is that what the meat in the icebox is for? What about getting some yoghurt to go with it, and I'll do you a Turkish dish, would you like that? Hell, we'll do it together, that'll be better. We'll do it together. Out of her loneliness and inertia Jane now found new energy, and Lyndall's enthusiasm for even the dreary household tasks was infectious.

Together they swept the flat and prepared the dinner, and Lyndall went down the street to buy flowers and yoghurt and Jane ironed the table napkins; and it was not serious, it was not like real life; it was like playing house. Yet Jane did not want the friends to come. Richard and Melissa. The world was all in couples. And one called them friends because they were couples, of about the same age. We'll ask the so-and-so's and the so-and-so's and then the so-and-so's will ask us back. Childless couples, or couples with babies, or couples with a child in nursery school; young professional men on their way up, young wives absorbed in pregnancies and child rearing and the right kind of school. Jane was ashamed, before Lyndall, of her world; wanted to explain, beforehand, I am not like them, the others, not really; I do not fit in here; I am like you, I want to be like you. She would have liked to have spent the evening with the doors closed and curtains drawn against the outside world, keeping Lyndall to herself. But Lyndall was playing, enjoying herself. With Alex in the bathroom shaving and washing, Lyndall pulled clothes out of the heap in her bag, crumpled magnificent dresses, a lace blouse, rainbow colours, embroidery everywhere. What shall I wear? You must wear your green dress, but which one do you think I should put on? She held up first a white shift like a nightdress, long and fine, with flowers embroidered on it as if they had been scattered at random. Then a velvet dress, purple, with floating sleeves. In a moment she had pulled her shirt over her head, dropped her pants and stood there quite naked. Jane felt a peculiar shock; that that was what being female could be like, so slight, so uninvolved. Lyndall's hair fell about her shoulders, bright golden, and her bare feet upon the carpet were long-toed, prehensile; there she was, complete and unselfconscious, preoccupied with choosing the right dress to put on over that nakedness, oblivious perhaps of the conflict of Jane's feelings. Jealousy, that Lyndall should be like that and she like this, so heavy, used. Admiration, as if she were a painting or a piece of sculpture. And the sudden thought that this was what it would be like to love another woman. There it was, the second unthinkable thought that she had had since Lyndall's arrival; the first, that Alex should make love to Lyndall; now, that it was possible for herself to feel like this. Lyndall pulled the purple dress on and it fell in long folds around her feet. She twisted up her hair with one hand and stuck in a pin, fixing it. There. Will that do? A look sideways to see the effect, that was suddenly conscious.

Aren't you going to wear anything underneath?

Well, I usually don't bother. No one's going to know, are they? Jane had the sudden intuition that nothing this evening would be what it seemed to be; that Richard and Melissa would be unexpected, different people; that Lyndall was capable, simply by being there, of transforming the world. She went to put on the new green velvet dress now, and brushed out her hair. Then she felt different, herself; relaxed, welcoming, even looking forward to seeing the other couple, whom she did not particularly like. When Alex came to find her, she saw that he too was lit by a certain expectation; and they looked at each other in surprise. Lyndall made it for me, she said; this morning. And he smiled his appreciation, his recognition that things had changed.

That evening. They would look back on it, the four of them, each couple separately, long after Lyndall had gone; and Jane would often think to herself, that was the evening when I first began to understand. The grilled lamb kebabs in their sauce of yoghurt and herbs, the salads that Lyndall had made, tasted surprising, a new taste. Lyndall told them that it was the cumin powder she had used; but Jane thought that it was her own ability to taste that had returned. They ate and drank and talked, leaning on the table, then moving to sit cross-legged or lounge against a chair leg on the floor. The white wine went down; but it was not that they were drunk, no, not just that. Understood what, then? That what Lyndall said was true for the moment; that one only had to feel affection towards somebody for that person to become lovable. What was it that had always irritated her about Richard, who lay on the floor now with his head on his wife's knee, who seemed this evening so fine-featured, so intelligent? She could not remember. And why had conversations with Melissa been so boring; was it that until now they had both only talked of themselves, their husbands' work, housework, the repetition of days? Alex, sitting between Lyndall and Richard, thought how very different Richard seemed at work, began to see a person there whom he had never glimpsed before; and he thought this even while feeling Lyndall's knee beside his and the long weight of her body against him on the sofa. He said something to Lyndall, that Jane could not hear. But she looked across at him and understood. She was connected suddenly to them both. Afterwards, she thought, there was a strong sexual link between all of us, that night; and knew that she would never discover what had happened once she had gone to bed. Yet the strangeness, the liveness of that evening was enough for her, and she went, leaving them all there, her husband and his colleague from work, the wife and the stray young American; and lay alone between her cool sheets obsessed with her own new feeling of sudden affection for the child that kicked and curled itself inside her. It was the first time. She knew now that she could love it, enable the child itself to love. For the first time, it was a person, sexless, as yet unidentified, yet potentially capable of love. She spread out her limbs to the four corners of the bed and fell instantly asleep. She did not hear any door shut or any car drive away; did not feel the weight of Alex come to change the level of the bed; awoke, in fact, alone, perfectly rested, and found that the calm and the pleasure were still there, when the child moved, that she could even imagine it waking up and stretching out its small fists as she did in the morning. In the kitchen, there was Alex, alone, drinking coffee. Without speaking to him, she looked around; suddenly afraid. Yes. The sheets and blankets were all folded, there was no Arab embroidery anywhere, the little box of marijuana and the hairbrush and the amber worry-beads were gone, and there was only the faint smell of her in the sitting room among the smoke and ash and warm smells of the evening before.

Alex said, she's gone. He was white and his eyes had that glitter still, they were clear and yet dark, distended as if he were looking at a brilliant point of light.

Jane said, what are we going to do? She meant, having to live without Lyndall.

Be different, said Alex; that's all. Come on, have some coffee, I'm just making some toast. There was the smell of burning toast and a little file of blue smoke from the toaster, but she did not heave up her bulk suddenly to see to it, as she might have done; she let him go, leisurely watching. It doesn't matter, she said. Scrape it out of the window.

He said, if one can change overnight. I don't know.

I'm afraid of it all going back to how it was before.

He said, but we didn't realise, did we? What we'd started. There's no going back on that.

She did not ask him what he meant; but holding him, sensed a warmth, a slight heat and languor of the body, inhaled a slight scent, felt something that she recognised but knew she need not name. There was nothing to do, but allow a silence to emerge and hold them both still. They stood like this, in the kitchen, allowing the present moment to become the past; and the pale sun broke through outside again and came and poured into the room, watery and yet warm; patterns on the table, shadows on the floor; the beginning of a new day.

A letter came from Lyndall. She was in Ibiza with her lover, Harry, having sold the car to buy a plane ticket from Spain. She was happy; she hoped that they were too. They would see each other again, sometime, somewhere, she did not know where. Life was pleasure and fear and change. She sent her love to their baby and hoped that it would have a good life. She loved them both. She was, as ever, theirs, Lyndall.

Sex in the Movies

First there was one body, then two, and then it seemed, one again, fitted with many arms and legs. But the girls were used to this, the cinematographic symbol of human love; just as other generations were used to lights dimming, flowers blossoming, a glance across a room, a study of bedroom furniture. They sat in a row and smoked their cigarettes or chewed gum. On the screen, the naked man groaned at last and flung himself away from his partner, so that they became once again two. The woman, on her back on the grass, lay with her face inscrutable. There was a shadow of armpit, of pubic hair. The man sat up, his thigh turned against the camera to hide his genitals; he seemed at a loss;

once, he would have drawn up a sheet and exhaled smoke from a cigarette. The drums grew louder on the soundtrack, a jazz rhythm. In letters with no capitals, the words grew across the screen, writing 'the end'.

'Not bad,' Angela said at once, gathering up bag, cigarettes, her glasses case, her short leather coat. They filed after her out into the aisle. Sylvia would have liked to wait, not to have to talk about it yet. It was like the moment at school, when the teacher asked one immediately what one thought about a piece of writing; she too was at a loss. In the foyer there was warm pink light and crowds waited, muttering, to go in. The posters flared across the walls, all that naked flesh. And one must have an opinion, it was decreed. 'It was fantastically real at the end.'

'How do you know?' asked Karen. The street was wet and lit with yellow light. They huddled, shrugging into their coats, dropping things.

'What d'you mean, Sylv?'

'Well, I just mean, the way it ended. Them coming together again.'

'You mean, the screwing?'

'Yes.'

'I thought he was good,' Maggie said. 'Nice eyes.'

'Nice —. Nice other things, too.' Karen spoke and they all giggled.

Angela said, 'She was a bit fat, though, wasn't she?'

'Just because you're so damn skinny. Some men like girls with a bit of fat.'

'Sylv would do. How about it, Sylv?'

'How d'you know it was real, Sylv?'

'Back of the bike sheds, that's how she knows. Has Gary Hollis got a big one, then?'

'Oh, shut up.' The thing about Gary Hollis, Sylvia thought, was that he never spoke, never intimated. He held her hand in a dry, firm grip; seeing this film made her wish that he would do more. But she was older than all of them, except Angela, and she would assert her experience. 'I thought we were talking about the film' she said, 'Not boring boys at school. Can't we have a rest from that, once in a while?'

'Oooh, listen to her.'

'Well. I'll be Miss Henderson. What did you think about that film, Sylvia? What — er — aspects of it particularly impressed you? Was it his big prick, or did you have some more intellectual thing to say? Tell the class, Sylvia.'

'Give us a ciggy, Mag, will you. If you really want to know, I thought it was a fantastic story. I mean, you never thought they were going to make it up at the end, did you? It seemed as if they were all washed up, he was so bored with her, and that.'

'Make it up? What are you on about?' Led by Karen, they all pounced. 'What d'you mean, make it up?'

'They weren't making it up.'

'Well, I mean, them making love at the end, it was hopeful, sort of. Made you think they were going to have a new start, that sort of thing.'

'Of course it wasn't, Sylv, it was to show how miles apart from each other they were, how they didn't understand each other at all. Like when he was mixing that drink, at the party, the look on his face. He hated her really.'

'But how can he have done, if he — ' She remembered tenderness, a hand going out. But had that been in the film?

'Well, he was just doing it to show how it wasn't any good, wasn't he? Otherwise he wouldn't have turned away right afterwards.'

'And she wouldn't have been on her back, just lying there.'

'It was just a habit, wasn't it, for them to do that after a party.'

'It was the director's way — ha, listen to this — it was the director's way of showing how relationships always end up like that. Married ones, I mean.' Angela ground her cigarette stub underfoot. 'Come on, let's move, we can't stand here all night. My Mum gets cross if I'm late.'

The pale figures receded in Sylvia's mind, became insignificant, grew again into others. The man came across the garden in the small hours after the party, a whisky glass still in his hand. He was unshaven, tired, his fine eyes bloodshot. The woman in her black dress stood under a tree and watched the beginnings of a sunrise. How was one to understand this in the complex pattern? A sunrise was a sunrise, a tree a tree. With Gary, in a sunrise, she would not look for other meanings. And yet in the English class there was talk of symbols, of things being other than as they seemed. Love was not love, sex not sex. 'It was just a habit, wasn't it, for them to do that after a party.' 'And she wouldn't have been on her back ....' There was a code, to be understood. The sunrise grew, spread up the sky. The man came near, at first he looked tired, defeated; but then one knew from something in his face, something no one had explained, that it was changing, it was growing and coming up. And then he put his hands on the woman in black and turned her towards him, and at that point Sylvia felt a sudden heat in her stomach and a trembling in her legs; then, not later, not at the point where he groaned and fell away. She did not think of Gary then, nor of meanings, but was turned to pure sensation, drawn into the film. Somehow, with great speed it seemed, the two had begun to undress each other; first the man's shirt, then the woman's dress, her petticoat; out fell two very white and pointed breasts, into his hands like eggs; then she bent to unzip his trousers, and off they came, and to her surprise he wore no underpants but was suddenly naked. Beneath all those trousers that one saw every day in the street, there was perhaps naked flesh. With the disappearance of bras, vests and underpants, life loomed closer and more dangerous. Miss Henderson at school said, 'Censorship is the imposition of one person's tastes upon another. Any mature person can choose what he does or does not want to see.

What is not within one's experience, one will not be able to understand.'

And the bodies became one, she felt that sudden entry, that working about inside. 'How do you know?' asked Karen. D. H. Lawrence wrote that there was a flame that grew down one's legs; she felt and located it precisely. The broad hands closed over the breasts, the narrow buttocks clenched and released, the man heaved up as in a spasm of pain and fell away again. The woman's face was inscrutable. The film ended before she could sit up and put on her clothes. There was the sunrise, and the words, 'the end.' She and her friends sat in a row, assessing technique, watching it all. Now they moved away down the street, stepping through the pools of lamplight, their faces yellow as they turned to argue.

Sylvia said, 'I still don't see. Why would they have done that if they hated each other?' For she must be told, outright in words, so that there was no mistake.

'Well, that's what being married is like, isn't it.' Angela spoke, and they were all silent, knowing that Angela's dad had left only last year.

'Not necessarily.'

'Well, it's what you hear all the time, isn't it. Anyway, who'd want to stay with the same bloke forever? You'd get sick of it, wouldn't you.'

'Only in the film it was the bloke that got sick of it.'

'Well, I'm not going to get married.'

'I'm going to have a gigolo. Always get them mixed up with gondolas, somehow. That is the right word, isn't it?'

Miss Henderson said, turning her beautiful face gently upon the class, 'You will find that the literature of the twentieth century deals mostly with the transience of love.' Transience. One did not dare to ask her what words meant, but looked them up in a dictionary in the library afterwards, because some of the words she used sent a shiver, like sex, through the spine.

Karen said, vigorously, 'You could tell, anyway, he fancied that blonde at the party. That was it, he was having his wife because he really wanted the blonde, only he couldn't have her because she was with that big bloke, you remember, in the summer house thing.' She twirled her shoulder bag, pleased with her interpretation.

Angela said, 'It was obvious he was going to fancy somebody else. You could tell how he was liking his wife less and less, all through the film. After that bit with the baby in the hospital, when she was crying, and he suddenly looked at her and saw how old and ugly she looked, with her mascara running everywhere.'

Maggie said, 'And then the bit where she asks him to unzip her dress when it gets stuck. You could tell he didn't really want to. He went and cleaned his teeth afterwards as if he had a nasty taste in his mouth.'

And Karen said, 'Then the bit at the party, when the wife doesn't know anybody and he has to take her and introduce her to people, you could see how bored he was with her. And people saying they were sorry about the baby, how that just turned him off.'

And Angela said, 'Well, he was a lot more sexy than she was, anyway.'

And Maggie said, 'The trouble with her was, she didn't know where to get off.'

They came to the turning where Sylvia's road branched off to the right, where Maggie had to wait for her bus. Together they stood, thoughtful and silent for a moment; and men in cars slowed down and leaned from their windows in the damp night, and sometimes called out. On fleeting celluloid, pale limbs twined and gripped each other, there was a sudden grating of flesh. Sylvia said, 'Goodnight, then. See you in the morning.'

'Goodnight, Sylv.'

'Cherrah.'

'See you.'

And standing in the narrow kitchen at her home, watching her mother cut and pack sandwiches for the morning, answering when her mother without looking up said, 'Good film, love?', Sylvia replied, 'Awful'.

A Bird Flew In

A bird flew into my room that morning, the morning of that day at school. The thud of his head on glass, the complicated sound of his wings as they beat against the walls, was in my dreams long before I woke. Waking was a struggling up through that sound, an attempt to rationalise it, an escape from fear. And I lay on my back, my bed close to the floor, the ceiling a long way up; the white walls of the room a narrow box. The curtains drawn partly back, my window sash pushed up, and the cold morning air, the watery sunlight, coming in. The bird had come in too; for that was what it must be, a bird, that flutter and crash, that thick block of the light that made me blink. My eyes followed him as he beat to and fro, to and fro, across my room, his prison. The rest of me could not move. I thought of birds' bodies, easily crushed; and of holding that wild heart in my hand. In a minute the wings would brush my face. Dead, dying, he would fall upon me. In my white bed, as the sun came in, I screamed.

I told her about it, when she came towards me on the way to school, swinging her shoe bag as she always did. We exchanged news, always. She danced about, in those days, as if her feet itched. This morning, they were in short red wellingtons, because of the rain in the night; the rain that I had sensed as soon as I awoke, from that gleam at my window, and the car sounds on the road. She seemed to be only half listening; jumping, hopping, swinging that bag about; but at the end she always knew what one had said. A bird? How weird. There was a film about that, I saw a bit on the telly, about hundreds of birds, all coming to get this person, and the girl rushing about, scared to death, trying to get away.

Yes. That was what it had felt like. But I said, it was only a robin.

What did you do, then? Did you shoo it out?

No, I didn't want to. My mum came. She got it out of the window.

Oh.

She was my friend, Monica, from the early days, when we were first there in Miss Hunter's class and just played. It was her crisp blond hair that first bound me to her, that and her way of jumping about; something so lighthearted there was about her, so energetic. One never knew what was going to happen next. She was exciting, she was volatile: she was daring; she was something I had not met in my life before. And now she said, come round my house after school? And the day changed colour once again. We ran up the glossy wet pavement. Autumn had something about it that made one want to snort and champ, like horses. The light changed, the day changed, it was all shifting, subtle, the street a world of patterns, the sky and the fields beyond hardly seen. Yes, I said, okay.

Monica's house was one in a row. Mine — my parents' — was on its own, a bungalow with white railings and hydrangeas in the garden. To go to Monica's you had to cross the main road by going over a high iron bridge with gaps in it and the traffic moving about like sharks underneath; coming down the steps on the other side, you had to step off suddenly into the sky. Then there was an alleyway, past the crisp factory, past the yard where the co-op vans parked, and into the street. Monica's street was full of shops and dogs and parked bikes and people standing in the road to talk. Whereas the street where our school was was only just made, and there were fields just beyond it, on the other side of the railway line. It had kerbs, houses, lamp posts; but looked to me always somehow unfinished, like a drawing where something has been left out and you have to guess what. We went down the street, stopping at the corner shop, painted puce and a sign outside, Get Your Bread Here. Monica had more money, always; she took it off the mantelshelf when her grandad was not looking, she pocketed the change from her dinner money herself. She bought sherbets, two lollies, packs of bubble-gum, and we went on. When she spoke to the shopkeeper she tossed her head like a pretty pony and she pouted, her lips very pink, making dimples appear. And he smiled after us, at her and not at me, while she led the way out, her legs very long now between the skirt and the red wellingtons, her pale blue coat flying open, button-less, too small, yet grand all the same. I followed. Something nagged at me, like a stomach ache, like something forgotten. It was that I had not gone home first, to say where I was going. They won't mind, Monica had said, pouting the way she did, not to be crossed; they won't notice, will they? Mine never do. Anyway, only babies have to say where they are all the time.

Past the house where the fat woman always stood in her doorway, smoking, an eye on the world; past the newspaper stand, headlines, schoolgirl found; past the beer lorry with its orange stacked boxes and the man with the squint who drove; past a row of bikes and two little kids playing conkers on the pavements; and we were at Monica's door. She ran up the alley at the side, her legs kicking out sideways. Shouted back at me, come on, I want to see if he's left any money, then we can go out. I followed. The brick walls were very close together. I was afraid of creeping in, of going to the mantelpiece, of Monica's grandad coming downstairs, very quiet in his bedroom slippers, opening the door quite suddenly, catching us there. I wished now that I had gone home. It was quite one thing being with Monica in school, where there were teachers, other people, where order ruled. Come on, silly. I went. There was the tangly little back garden and the brick place where the toilet was, wet toilet roll coming out under the door. Their cat sat under a wet bush and looked at us, yellow-eyed. Monica kicked open the back door, ran in, shouted out loud, grandad! I was used to this, to her empty house, or the old man sitting in his corner by the low fire, mostly unaware. Ever since we were five or six, when I had come here, there was this mystery about the house. There was nobody really there; and yet it felt full. Always as if somebody might come upon one suddenly, unawares. I stood by the door, nervous. The fire smoked. Monica said, he must have gone down for his paper, come on, look, here's four bob; two each. Let's go. We banged the door, ran. Into the suddenly darkening street, the onset of winter, each with our coin. I forgot, then, that I should be home; there was only the gleam of her head as it bobbed in front, and the clop-clopping of her shoes on the pavement and the space before us, dusk and lights and houses. We stopped at the off-licence first and bought crisps and a bottle of coca-cola to share. Then there was the decision, where to go, where to have it. Down to the right were the narrow streets that were all called after fruit, Apple Street, Pear Street, Medlar Street, left from the days when there were orchards here, that led to the canal. Dark-red, used brick now, old streets already, houses stacked close and only the number to show you which was which. Indian children rolling marbles into the gutter; the brown-white gleam of their eyes as we passed, and luminous socks marking the dusk. Nig-nogs, Monica said automatically as we passed; and I said automatically, Miss Hunter said we shouldn't say that.

Miss Hunter! Who cares?

Well, you wouldn't like it.

You are a mardy-bum, Jeannine.

The canal was black as liquorice, shadowed by warehouse buildings that were palaces in the water. My hand touched stone, after warmer brick. Let's sit here, shall we, Monica said, and then no one'll see us. We perched side by side on the slanting stone coping of a little wall, our legs dangling. Opened crisp packets with our teeth, prised off the coca-cola top that the off-licence man had loosened. Monica said, sometimes I have some of her sherry. When me grandad's out. The coca-cola was black and metallic against one's teeth, as if rot began at once. The bottle top dropped through thick air to the water beneath. It was a time that I loved, that day, with a frame round it, even then; set apart perhaps from my extraordinary wakening, when the bird had pounded against the glass in my room. Monica said, you are my best friend, aren't you?

Yes, of course I am. It was a fact, that I knew already. Monica and Jeannine are best friends. Miraculously, it had been long established.

I want you to be my best friend for ever. Will you give me something I can keep for ever? And then I'll give you something, I don't know what yet, but something, and you can keep it forever.

That day, for ever.

It grew darker. It was hard to see her clearly; only her eyes shone, and her cotton hair, and the smooth bone of her knee turning to the white of sock. The bottle gleamed and splashed into the canal, and the spray was metallic too. It is easier to see her as she is now, veins and scuffed wedge heels, wheeling those two in the high wire basket round the co-op; easier than to remember her exactly as she was, that evening.

And then I'll give you something, and you can keep it for ever. As if suddenly a fear of the future touched her; or was it the rising cold from the water in autumn, the damp of evening?

I said, you can have my bracelet, if you like. My birthday present, silver; I could see already my mother's face, but anything but what I most prized would not do. It too gleamed, changing hands; and on her wrist it was more beautiful. I thought, if what she gives me isn't enough, then I can say on Monday that me Mum says. But the thought died, unworthy of that time. A couple was coming down the road, where we had come, a man and a woman going down to the very banks of the canal, and Monica's elbow was sharp in my ribs; if we were very still they might not see us; but even the crisp packets sounded like a forest of dead leaves as we held our breath.

Monica whispered, at last, look! Down in the shadows, where they had turned left from the road, twenty yards from us, on the other side. Something white appeared, dropped. It's Irene, from up the shop, Monica whispered, I swear it is. Sssh. My elbow returned the nudge. Our eyes, through the thick twilight, saw only the changing shape of the shadow within the shadow; but we guessed, we knew, we put together all the hints we had ever had, one a week perhaps through the whole of our lives. The shadow heaved like one thing breathing. Up against the wall, by the canal. Every night perhaps. In and out, up and down, a few quick jerks, a long cry quickly smothered; and I thought of that bird, for some reason, the terrifying fragility, that beat in the palm of the hand. I had not touched it. My mother it was who had opened the window, let it fly. But I knew.

Monica said, standing up? As if something in her, some expectation, had been ended.

I remember that, her voice suddenly a bit pathetic, as if she minded. Then she said, practical, they mustn't see us, come on, we've gotta go. And we ran, scattering crisps, back up the way we had come, and saw two faces turn bright white dials suddenly towards us, and a hand raised, and heard somebody cry behind us, somebody made suddenly quiet; and did not stop until we had reached the street, where Monica lived. The street was bright, noisy after that quiet place, and it suddenly was much later in the evening than we knew. There were people going in and out of the Feathers on the corner, and the shops had down their blinds. Christ, Monica said. Her hand up to run through her hair, and my silver bracelet slipping back up her arm. You better come back to my house, then my grandad won't — I never knew whether she was beaten at home, or not. There was always her look of fear, quickly conquered by gaiety, as she walked up the alleyway to her back door. Okay, I said; having no idea now what else I should do, my parents' house being in another world. And it was, it had always been, the source of my knowledge that two worlds existed; Monica's house. As a small child, going up to Monica's tiny bedroom to play, I knew that I was in a different world. It was not that it was poor, dirty, cramped, no; at five one hardly knows these things; but it was other. It was the first other. Now it waited for me, as I came up the street with Monica, four years later; now it was the only place left to go. She went up the alley before me, her jaunty walk, accentuated, and coat tails flying back. Ducked under the washing line, skirted the brick toilet, kicked open the door as she always did. And my bravado, being homeless, had to echo hers. The cat ran out from the back door, ears flat, and flew into the bushes. The room was full of smoke. It billowed out from the back door into the cold damp air. Monica stepped back, flapped her arms. Fire, she said, help, what shall we? And began to cough, her eyes streaming. But after a minute or two the smoke was not so thick, and we pushed our way in, through the door, simply because there was nobody behind us, nobody else to ask. Monica turned a white face, in which her eyes shone with water. It's me grandad, she said to me, quiet.

What?

I think he's dead. It must have been the smoke. Choked him. Or he died, and the fire began to smoke. I don't know. Whatever shall we do?

We opened the windows, calm as adults, not looking at what was behind. We stamped out the coals that had begun to smoulder on the damp mat. We took a saucepan of water and poured it on the fire, and flapped the rest of the smoke out through the back door. At last the room was cold and clear. Then we looked at Monica's grandad, where he sat in his usual place in the worn old armchair close to the fire. He looked the same as ever; for he never used to speak when we came in. His hands, rheumaticky, lay upon his knees like bits of wood. It was their colour I noticed first. And then you could see it in his face, something mottled, something wooden, happening as you looked. And his eyes were closed, and the lids dark, and nothing moved at all, there was no lift to his waistcoat, not the slightest thing. But I was not really frightened, not entirely surprised. He had always seemed more alarming when he was alive; being like somebody who looked dead, and then suddenly spoke. I realised that he was what had filled Monica's house, had made it feel full and that now it was empty. I looked around me, at the sudden emptiness. But she began, quite suddenly, to scream. As if she was putting it on, only I knew that she was not. It was just another sort of crying, that I had never seen before. She went rigid, and her face changed, changed shape, and her mouth went square and she began to scream. I took hold of her. I had to. I shook her and begged her to stop, and all the time the old man sat there in the armchair beside us, and could almost have been listening and not bothering to get up. Monica twisted and screamed and wriggled to escape me, and she was strong. I had her wrists, her hands groping at the air. It was a fight; and I had to make her stop. I twisted her left wrist, shouted, if you don't stop I'll take it, I'll take it back for ever! The silver bracelet warm and malleable in my hand. She stopped screaming quite suddenly, and began to cry ordinarily, scrubbing at her eyes and cheeks with the back of her hand. We were quite alone, and Monica was suddenly a baby, crying. I was dizzy with what I ought to do; all gravity gone wrong, all balance lost. Telephone. Somebody. But there wasn't one. Down the street. I said, I'd better go and — but she clutched at me, sobbing, don't go, you can't go, you mustn't go, you won't, promise me you'll stay here for ever. For ever. I snapped the clasp of the bracelet shut for her, so that it would not fall off her arm. There were footsteps coming up the alleyway, there was another person, anybody, on the way. I knew that in a minute I, too, would begin to cry. And she clung to me, Monica did, clung so close that our breathing, our crying, were joined, so that we had one shape and would have had one shadow.

That day had many sides; many lights; a particular colour of autumn, the wet gleam of the canal; the smell of school and the smell of Monica's house; smoke billowing into the black, wet garden; that suddenly empty house; her hair, as she sobbed, in my mouth. I was taken home. In a car by somebody strange. Given a pill and put to bed. So that only so much later did I get out that day in its wholeness and look at it again. The day on which I first saw sex and death, and on which a bird flew in through my window. At the time, and for so long afterwards, all I felt was the jolt against me of Monica's crying, and the sharp bones of her chest, and the river that poured simultaneously from both our eyes; and the clear sensation, known for the first time then, of another person's heart leaping under one's hand, against one's self; that certain caged flutter, that beat.

Horsemen

They came down one by one but close; one jangling bit close to another's tail, flanks sometimes just touching, a community of hot breath; fine horse, expensively bred, somebody's hunters out to exercise in the morning air. And he had seen them, oh, almost every morning since he started to come this way; sometimes tiny, they were, in silhouette moving on the ridge of a hill, sometimes smart as conkers in sunlight on the verge of the road. Four horses, four riders.

In front, the black horse with the man sitting very upright and holding his reins with one hand as if they might break; behind and around him the smaller bays and chestnut and the blond boy and two girls riding them. They were a faint clatter on the road far ahead, a sudden gleam of light, a puff of steam from a damp spinney; they awaited him, each morning they appeared somewhere along his road, conjured from the black plough and rich grazing land of the midlands country, he came to expect them, he drove carefully up to them and past, not to frighten the horses; after a couple of weeks the riders smiled at him and waved, and he waved back with a motorist's preoccupied lift of the hand.

For months he drove this road, choosing the narrow country way instead of the main road into town, meeting only farm traffic, tractors and carts. He came to drive in the middle of the road, confidently knowing each curve and bend and hidden rut, and where pheasant or partridge might run out, a tractor start from a lane, or a dog come from a thicket, hunting. Driving to work in the town, he became a countryman by proxy. From behind the glass and metal of his car, he saw mist break upon fine mornings, crops grown and harvested, perfected or ruined by weather, hayricks and potato clamps built and used up, logs gathered to sell, manure carted, stubble burned. He saw the horsemen like a daily proof of man's per-fectability. And his mind began to shrink from his job in the town until only the drive to work, the solitary half hour in the old Morris Minor, contained the day's meaning.

Arriving in town, he held his breath and submerged himself. It was only in the open countryside, where the ridge road wound between copse and plough and a church spire stood thin as a pencil, fields away, that he breathed and saw. The car held him like an incubator still, for he was not yet strong enough to be released from its climate. In winter the wind scraped the landscape bare, blackbirds flew low across the road, the yards were clogged with mud; it was in the winter that he began his pilgrimage, it was in the following autumn that it ended.

"How's it going, love?" His wife, Anne, stayed at home and looked after their new baby, and he felt that she only asked out of politeness. He came in flushed with the cold air and warmed his hands at her cheeks but she drew back, having been all day indoors.

"Same as usual."

"It's a pity you have all that driving now. It was so much easier for you at the flat." They had moved from the town flat and bought the cottage because of the baby; although Tom felt, looking at the baby, that she should not care where she lived, having everything she needed within reach. People had babies and moved to the country, and husbands drove to and fro.

Soon Anne would tire of this close hearth and would need work and a car too. The organic thing, the growth they had begun, would spread and grow around them like those plants that Anne had begun to grow in the kitchen. He could not tell how he felt about it. At present he was numb, and this shocked him. As a husband, as a father, one must feel. But all that remained was the sense of unreality, as soon as he got out of his car.

"It's okay, I like the driving. It gives me time to think. It's a beautiful drive."

"The main road?"

"I don't go by the main road, I go round by the ridge road and join the main road at Tanby."

"But that's miles further."

"But it's a nicer road."

"But it's so twisty. It must take you hours. Besides, you have to drive about five miles in the wrong direction first." He could tell that it disturbed her, that he should go the long way round. He frowned and stared at the fire, assessing all those unnecessary hours he had spent away from her. She said, "You must use an awful lot of petrol."

"Not all that much. Anyway, you said you were sorry I had so much driving; you ought to be pleased I've found a way I enjoy."

She said, "Let's talk about something else, shall we?" in her final, cheerful voice.

"Well, okay. What have you been doing?" Love, what was love? It was care, it was the line of anxiety on her smooth fair skin. It was their two heads, blond and black, bowed with responsibility while they were still young. It was the square red mouth of the infant that opened suddenly demanding all they had.

"Nothing much. It's been so cold. I didn't want to take her out, so we stayed in." As simple as that. Their igloo, their nest in a cold world. He yawned suddenly and said, "Can I have a cheese sandwich? I'm starving." And moved to cut the bread himself, a tall thin young man with knuckles still red from driving without gloves, his thick black hair flopping forward as he cut and spread; in his head the horsemen still waited upon the ridge road, the next day and the next; it was either this knowledge or the sudden comfort of food that made him turn to her and smile with new energy and begin again.

* * * * * *

Winter grew into a black and rainy spring, and even when snowdrops and crocuses began to appear, clouds made the hilltops dark, water streamed down the roads and ditches, flattened the fields, soaked the slabs of plough. The baby Justine grew fast and drew all her mother's attention to herself. In her dark hair and eyes, pursed mouth, grasping broad hands, Tom saw himself and was surprised at it; he had expected the baby to be like Anne, so that he would live with two calm blonde women through his life, and be looked after. This Justine was all passion and dissatisfaction, she raged against life and beat and tugged at it with her hands. At night she screamed until one of them stumbled through the darkness to her cot and found the lost dummy that would close her lips. An hour later she awoke, found the dummy gone, and screamed.

Dawn came in cold and late and there was an hour before Tom must leave for work. A strong pain linked the two parents and yet they lay hating each other because the other would not get out of bed. The baby's screams were like a rasp on metal. They knew that the baby was stronger than they, that she would not give up. Tom at last stood at her cotside and felt his hands and and wrists heavy with incipient violence. It was impossible that he should so hate his daughter, who was small and helpless, and so he hated in a void. Warming the bottle, changing the nappy, holding the strong dark head up to suck, he felt murder rise in his stomach. There was only the surface tenderness, the thin web of convention, morality, fear, to restrain him. If she screamed once more after this, he would pick her up, he would swing — but the block in his mind came down, shutting out the unthinkable, and he walked lightheaded and faint back to his wife and almost fell upon the bed.

The room was filled with grey light and Anne lay on her back, snoring with a sound like a sob. He heard the child whimper where he had laid her down in her cot, he waited to hear the next sound, the ascending roar or the quietening, sleepy suck, with a tension that seemed about to split him. He was there, spread out as if praying, his head buried in the blanket, his hands spread out to grip the bedclothes for control, when he saw the horsemen. They stood poised in his mind in the darkness of his inner eye, as they had so often stood upon the hill. Rain poured from the darkened coats of the horses as it poured into the cottage garden outside, into a world already saturated. They stood with their heads slightly bent, resting yet alert, and the steam from their nostrils made a cloud around them, around the quiet figures of the riders, the slippery hot flanks, the black soaked leather of the tack.

He saw the leader, the man upon the black horse, he felt rather than saw the grip of the man's thighs upon the power of the horse, holding him just in check; he wanted to cry out, stop, don't move, let me understand you; but the room lightened, the horses were gone, he was left spread and exhausted, quite limp again. The baby in the next room was quiet. The carpet as he rose seemed to hover at his knees like mist. Anne turned and woke and said, "Tom? Is she all right? Tom, come back to bed." An hour was left to him, less than an hour now. Greedily he fell back into sleep, as if he would devour its essence.

* * * * * *

There were days, as the weather grew warmer and blossom whitened the deep hedges at the sides of the ridge road, when the trotting horses on the tarmac appeared ordinary, a part of a sunlit world. He drove with his window rolled down and waved to them, the four people, quite casually. One day his daughter smiled at him, a first real conscious smile; at night she slept more as a human being sleeps, relaxed in her small cot. The awful, the fiendish quality seemed about to leave her completely, so that she might grow peacefully like anybody else. Only at times did her cry of rage and fear remind him, and he was struck as he watched the contorted face clear and settle, by the memory of a bad dream.

Anne began to take the child for walks, wheeling her under slowly greening trees. It seemed at last that they were not isolated, not damned. And spring became summer, and the whole landscape on fine mornings spoke to him of beauty and peace. Work was still an irrelevance, the hours still submerged; but he drove home in lengthened twilight and received the purple shadows on the land like a blessing.

Anne said to him, "It's good now, isn't it?" They would have a holiday, they would go away together, the three of them, and be happy as he and Anne had once been happy alone. On the last day before the holiday, he met the four riders coming up a slight incline before a bend in the road, and their movement in the heat of the July day was only the seal set upon his own happiness; it was as if they moved so surely because of the fullness of his own heart, as if he in his power had created them. He slowed right down, his arm hot upon the rolled down window, and as he passed them called out, "Lovely day, isn't it?"

The three stable hands, boy and girls, smiled and waved, and the man in front half-turned in his saddle to acknowledge the words; but said nothing and only raised his crop, as usual, in greeting. For the first time, Tom saw his face clearly, in strong sunlight, every line and curve apparent. He was dark, gipsy-dark, this man; thin, longboned; his hands gathered in his horse with tenderness; all this Tom had seen before. But in this moment at which all was stilled, birds silent, countryside inert, horse poised, man turned to face him, Tom saw a face so like his own that he felt his cheeks hot with recognition and inexplicable shame. The man, too, saw, recognised, understood and was amused; a smile that was no longer impersonal lightened his features, and he touched his horse with his heels as Tom touched the car's accelerator, and both moved on.

"I've got a double," was what Tom said to himself, moving from the empty country road to the main road into town "How peculiar. But of course, it does happen. I expect it happens all the time." But, how should he so know himself? His glance in the mirror in the morning was always perfunctory, accompanying a brief shave with an electric razor; otherwise, he never studied his own face at all. He would even admit that he did not really know what he looked like. Thin, yes, dark, yes; a particular combination of eyes, nose and mouth; and yet when he looked at the man on the horse he saw more than just that, knew more; he was looking at himself, knowing himself, for the first time.

And yet, there was the holiday to think of. There was travel, plans, shared excitement. There must be a real, exterior life which was fact and experience, to deny the power of this interior knowledge which weighed upon him, yes, which suddenly weighed him down. The shining rounded rumps of the four horses, black, chestnut and two bays, were gone round a bend in the road. Dark green leaves cast a shadow on the road, patterned the eye. The distance was blue, a summer darkness. Gnats hung in clouds under the great trees, chestnut and oak. Coming out into the harsh unshaded light, joining the traffic stream upon the burning main road, he said that he would come this way in future, that in the autumn he would drive this way to work.

* * * * * *

Yet in the early autumn a vision persisted in his brain; of the road, its hedges lit with dew on cobwebs, milk churns in solid silver waiting in the sun outside the farms, grey trees colouring slowly on their under sides as the mist lifted and September light turned the hills and fields white. The landscape drew him back, promising him a new side of itself; blackberries, rose hips in the hedges, sleek cats scuttling touched with sun away into the cool and empty yards; golden lying corn, houses built of the pale stooks, straws from a passing harvester scattered in the roadway. He thought of the horsemen for the first time in weeks; first, cold light drawing fire from a bit, a stirrup; then the breath in the chill air, the warmth of the horses' mouths as they tugged to go faster, the damp patches drying on their flanks as the sun warmed them, as the air about them turned a chalky blue.

And one day he simply turned his car in the old direction and set off up the ridge road again. In a high field where the straw was stacked in a crenellated tower, shadows moved upon the stubble. Blackbirds were cruising low and a black horse cantered over the cropped straw. The black horse and his rider were out alone this morning, circling and circling the field; the horse's ears pricked against hard sunlight, breath pumping steam, hoofs turning up mud clods to fly through the air; the canter was even, controlled, and the man not the horse was the controller. Invisible larks shouted, the earth seemed to breathe; silence rested upon a dim roar.

Tom sat and heard his own heart, that mechanism. And suddenly he could sit there no longer but must get out of the car — slamming the door to let the man know and the horse falter — and stand at the gate, chin and hands on the cold damp wood, watching them. The wood was soft, porous. The earth in the field smelled of cold, straw, dung, an autumn smell; there was smoke from a wood fire, there was the warm horse and the cold smelted iron of his shoes. Tom opened his mouth and let the air rush in like a draught of cold water, filling his throat, lungs and stomach with pleasure. All these weeks, these months of travelling past this spot, and he had never dared to stand here and breathe in this air but had moved past, encased in metal; and now he stood relaxed, forgetting all else, and watched his horseman ride.

At home in the cottage they began to burn wood fires, and sit close with hot drinks in the evenings. Tom sat opposite Anne, like an old friend who has nothing to say, and she smiled and talked to him and gave away nothing. Upstairs in her cot, Justine stood and hurled objects to the floor, bang, bang, one thing after another, they heard her and sat in a wrecked silence. Then she began to rattle the bars and bang her head against the cot end; like a dog at its kennel, Tom thought; and the screams of anguish began.

The neat, low cottage, the garden with its roses and hydrangeas, the life they led now had been for her. She would grow up among pleasant things as they had wanted her to; yet upstairs she howled like a young wolf, rejecting them all, threatened them from her place in the pink and white nursery upstairs, where the mobiles swayed above her and the alphabets and bright pictures hung on the wall. Alone, she howled and banged her misery; and downstairs, in the room which Anne had carefully tidied after the ravages of the day, her parents sat and talked to each other politely.

"But it's no good giving in."

"But there must be something wrong, or she wouldn't."

"Children can blackmail you."

"I just think she doesn't like us."

"She doesn't seem to me to like anything."

"I do hope she'll grow out of it. You've no idea what it's like being with her all day."

"No." In the mornings, immediately after breakfast, he escaped to his lonely road, leaving her. For the first time he ached, at not having told her. "When I drive to work," he paused, "you know the ridge road? Well, when I drive along it in the morning I always see some people out exercising horses. Hunters. There are always the same four people and one of them, a man, always rides a black horse. I always look out for them. Anne?"

"Well, it's a horsy part of the world."

"There's something about them. Something beautiful."

And she looked up, bit a thread, warning him with her glance. He said, goaded, "Well, one has to have something in one's life — " The room about them fell dark, colder; upstairs the child screamed for attention.

"I'd better go to her."

"No, I'll go. You've had her all day."

"No, she's more used to me, she'll play you up."

He said, when she was out of the room, "She's my daughter too." And remembering a night when his hand had been stayed from unthinkable violence, thought that that moment, at least, had given him a right. But he stayed where he was out of inertia, watching the low fire and the shadows upon the carefully painted walls. When Anne came back, her face relieved of her longing to control her daughter, she was almost gay. "She's settled down. I think it must have been wind. I gave her some of that gripe water, it seemed to do the trick in no time. Sorry, Tom, what were you saying? About the horses?"

"Nothing. I mean, there was nothing more to tell."

"Oh." Her life continued without him, he was irrelevant, the things that he saw did not concern her. Her small 'Oh', so easily satisfied, hurt him still.

* * * * * *

And the next morning was yet more brilliant, clearing in minutes out of a thick mist, as if a curtain drew back across the sky. On the ridge road, when he stopped the car and opened the door to get out and look and breathe his first breath, there were woodpigeons in the trees, the browned leaves lifted slightly in the air, the fields were vast, bleached, scarred only where night fires had burned the stubble black. He stood still and waited to hear the horses' hoofs. And so tuned, so accurate had he become, that within minutes he heard them strike and clatter on a distant stretch of road, come nearer, breast the hill all at once, four in a row and breathing like bellows, iron slipping on tarmac, bone jarring the earth.

He stood and watched them come like a man in a dream; and then on an impulse turned and began to stride on up the road as if he would never drive again. A pulse beat in his head, he grew warm, he lifted his arms and pumped blood through his body with the movement and raised his head to the sun. The trotting horses came closer behind him, ringing echoes in the air; a dog barked and barked in an invisible yard; the horses came level, the man on the black horse closest, holding in muscle beneath a dampened skin; he waved his greeting and the sun came down in a flash, a jay fell screaming between branches, dipped and rose; scared, the black horse skidded, reared back from the unknown in his path and the flecked spittle flew from his mouth into Tom's face; a figure slipping drew a black parabola against gold branches and the horse's forefeet came down in a dangerous iron curve, the last Tom saw before the vision cracked over like ice on a pond and he lay unconscious, at last, of all that passed.

How may one end the story of a longing, an obsession so clumsily fitted to the demands of real life? For the dark-faced groom was not seen in the neighbourhood again. Tom Meade's life went on; he sat with his head bandaged and his arm in a sling and watched his calm wife tame the child, and the child, her face cleared of its torment, smile and play and grow. It was only the black horse, its knees broken upon concrete, that had to be shot.

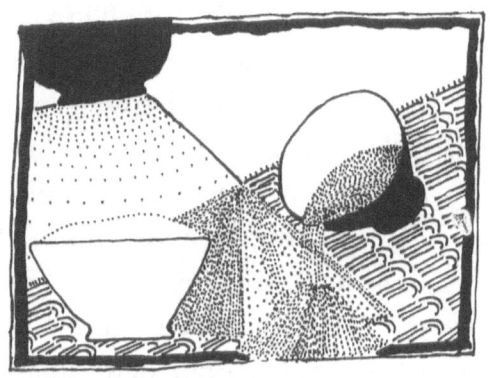

One in a Thousand

In another place, another time, she would not have been remarkable; a woman approaching middle age, grey hair drawn back unbecomingly, shoulders slightly rounded, upper arms plump where the sleeves of her dress droop against them. That is how she is seen from behind, by those sitting behind her. She is not ugly, not outrageous; not like the photographs they would have recognised in magazines, pictures of poverty or misery. A woman standing outside a shack in South America: a photographer can tell you what to feel. But there is nothing about her that gives them the cue for compassion. Nobody has told them. They only are aware of her, her difference, her unacceptability. They see a dowdy woman — 'obviously took no trouble with herself at all' — with a small boy — 'shockingly out of control' — in the stalls of a brand new theatre in a town in south-east England. But they feel. Oh, yes. Anger, resentment. Hatred. Their eyes dart hatred at her back. She knows it, she feels it. Her shoulders droop under its impact. She will not turn her head lest they see that there are tears in her eyes.

The play is a children's play, 'The Pied Piper of Hamelin', in which all children are spirited away, as the rats of the town have been; all except one crippled boy, who is left behind. The story is not important. What matters is that our children watch with discreet interest what happens on stage, and smile, and clap. When the chief actor calls out to the audience, as he always must in a children's play — 'Clap your hands! Shout after me!' our children must clap for the right amount of time, shout in unison, display the right amount of animation and no more. But what is happening? What *is* that child in the fourth row up to? What *can* his mother be thinking of, letting him go on like that? Once might be considered funny, but more is plain ill manners. Calling out like that, making a disturbance, upsetting the other children. It shouldn't be allowed. She should have more control over him. Some women have no idea. Be quiet, be quiet! Can't you control your own child? This will have to stop. You will have to go. We will have to call the management. This cannot go on. Will you kindly keep that child quiet?

'Jason', she said, 'Jason, sit down.' Oh, it was no use, what was the good of telling him? She only did it for their sakes, so that they would hear that she tried. 'Jason, you're making too much noise.' But he sprang up on his seat, he bounced with excitement, he called out with all the force of his lungs to the man on stage, 'You can't see what I can see! Hey, look out mister, there's another rat! You never caught all them rats, did you?'

And the man on stage, the actor, only in it out of desperation — a man almost permanently out of work, who put on his pied suit in the afternoons as if putting on overalls for a boring job — he was momentarily taken by surprise. The audience had been so predictable, the middle-class children, the controlling mothers and teachers. But the child was not going to stop, not until he got a response. The actor stood, listening, a stuffed rat in his hand. His face composed itself into an expression of jolly complicity; all he could do now, to make it seem as if he could cope, was to encourage the child. Make it seem intentional, give the audience a laugh. He called back to the little boy, after too long a pause in which the child grew almost hysterical with frustration, 'Go on, then. Tell us where all the rats are. Anybody else see any more rats? Or is it just this young gentleman here?' The rest of the audience murmured, remained still. Children twisted to look at their mother's faces, to see if this might be accepted. Jason rose in his seat again, yelled, 'You didn't really take all them old rats away!

'Did'.' said the Piper. He gambled, and lost.

'Didn't.'

'Did.'

'Didn't.'

'Did.' The audience grew restive; mothers and grandmothers began to frown.

'Didn't!' yelled Jason, set to go on all night. And, 'Jason', his mother implored, 'Jason, please.'

The Piper's annoyance began to show in the exaggerated listening stance he took, his face was all strained tolerance. And this was only the bloody matinee.

The voices began to tug at her as she had tugged, in vain, at her Jason. Shouldn't be allowed, ought to know better, ought to be stopped; they rose about her like inevitably deepening water, and she sat with her face held above it, trying not to inhale the flood. A person about to drown; this was how she often saw herself. Only just holding herself above the water. And now a voice addressed her directly, she had to turn her head a little and take notice of it. Inside her head a rhythm beat: I won't go out, I won't go out. The kind, patient voice of the woman who represented 'the management' said to her now, 'I'm afraid there've been some complaints. I'm afraid if you can't keep him quieter you'll have to take him out.' Fussy old cats, the girl was thinking, who had been sent on this errand. 'What's the theatre for, if not for kids to enjoy themselves? Some people'd do anything just to make a fuss.' But she said what she had to say, 'I'm afraid you'll have to take him out.'

'I'll try. I'm sorry.' She knew that a tear slid along her nose, was about to drop. She fumbled in her bag for the tube of fruit gums she had brought, her last weapon in the armoury of entreaty, threat and bribe. He took the tube from her absently, ripped the paper off the top, began popping the sweets into his mouth in quick succession, not taking his eyes from the stage. It would not last more than a few minutes. But the actor saw his chance, twirled with relief before the audience, began again to intone his lines. The children, quickly diverted to watch what they were supposed to watch, involved themselves again with the play; it was, after all, the theatre, a treat. Only a wary adult eye wandered towards Jason as he stood there, munching, staring, his head erect upon his bare stalk of a neck, the rigidity of his back expressing a readiness to spring into action. There was no reason to think that he would not begin all over again in a minute; some of the well-made-up faces under some of the waved and tinted heads of hair let slip a secret hope that he would, so that their indignation could run its course. And she sat, waiting, aware of them. She was so used to it now that the whole episode was like a scene in a play whose words and actions were inevitably the same against a series of different backgrounds. Trains. Bus stations. The playschool they had tried. Other people's houses. Supermarkets. The doctor's waiting room. And why had she not foreseen this, how could she not have been certain that it would all happen again? But the play on stage was, thank God, coming to an end. Jason had finished his sweets and screwed up the paper and hurled it into the aisle, he was shouting and chanting now against the burst of final music, but such a riot of music and dancing was there on stage now, that his small figure and even his voice made no real impact. The Pied Piper, the rats, the children, the townspeople in their strangely medieval clothes, all were circling in a kind of frenzy, before their final bow; Jason's ecstatic singing rose and wavered above the confident stridency of a pseudo-operatic score. Love had triumphed. Avarice was vanquished. Childish innocence and honesty had won. The Piper, thinking now of his gin-and-tonic in the dressing-room, took his last bow alone; and the children, the mothers, clapped. She could not clap. The physical effort of raising her hands from her lap would be too much. She was not sure if she would be able to stand up. Perhaps this, after all, was to be the last time; the last straw — the moment at which she cracked. One did crack some time, one could not go on like this. And as the theatre audience began to rise and shuffle out, pick programmes and bags from the floor, hunch into coats, shepherd children, set faces patiently towards the doors, she sat in her seat and wept. Beside her, Jason bounced on the seat and chanted and waved his programme. The passing mothers and grandmothers in their well-cut winter afternoon dresses looked at him with pity and curiosity as well as distaste. The poor child; how could he know any better? It was the mother's fault. She should be able to control her child, that was where she had failed. It was against her, not Jason, that the criticism was set. Making a scene in public. Sitting there crying. No self-respect. And she wept on and on and would not move, not until she was sure that they were gone.

'Excuse me.' Was that a voice that intruded? 'Excuse me. I just wondered — ' She looked up, knowing how she appeared; streaked face, red eyes, straggly hair. The girl's face was unknown to her; was she asking her something? 'I just wanted to say, they were making a fuss about nothing. Some people just love making a fuss. I shouldn't worry about them.' But who was this girl, that she could speak with such scorn of all those well-dressed, well-fed, well-adjusted people? Of the woman in the red wool trouser suit who had sat just behind, with her three blond children, the girls in velvet, the boy in his flowered shirt, and the older woman, the grandmother, who had tapped her first peremptorily on the shoulder so that she was aware of a perfume at the back of her, an educated voice, a hand weighted with rings and authority? How could one dismiss them so lightly? They were the ones who ordered this world. She stared at the face of the girl, watched her as she suggested impatiently a cup of tea 'to cheer you up, after those harpies'. In the stalls, now, they were picking up paper, programmes, crumbs, dusting the seats down for the next performance. The presence of the heavy red curtains made everything hushed. Jason's mother said in a whisper, 'Yes, all right, that would be lovely. Wouldn't it, Jason?' Jason stared and then let out a whoop, chilling as that of a tropical bird. The girl looked at him casually, 'How old is he?'

'He's only four. It's the first time he's been at a play, you see. He gets ever so excited.'

'Did you enjoy it, then, Jason?' There was something practiced in her voice, something habitually maternal.

'Smashing', said Jason.

'Rebecca thought it was a bit boring, didn't you, love? But it was her first time, too. But I'd no idea they still put on such dreary stuff for kids, had you? I wouldn't have brought her.'

For the first time, she noticed the child, a little girl smaller than Jason, clinging to the corner of her mother's wool smock, her other hand at her mouth. She nodded, but said nothing. She wore a short, bright red dress, black tights with a small hole at the knee, and her hair, like her mother's, was cropped short. They both had a bright, quick look, like little animals. And as they moved towards the door in front of her and Jason, she could see that the mother too was tiny, not more than five foot three, and wore nothing more elegant than blue jeans and sneakers and the faded, flowery smock. She had dismissed the rich women of the town with a gesture, she had dismissed the play. 'Dreary stuff.' 'Harpies.' The child with her picked her nose and was not rebuked. How did one come by such confidence? Jason's mother followed her, and Jason for once was silent at her side. And as they passed the people in the canteen, all eyes came up to look not at the girl with her casual clothes and her air of easy belonging, but at the woman who followed her, grey hair pulled back into a ponytail style too young for her, worried blue gaze, dress that was the wrong length and a poor fit — and at the bright-eyed prancing boy at her side, who was like a small dog straining continually at the lead. For about the first two there was nothing strange; their ease of manner, that of the young mother with her child, was the ease of a whole gifted moneyed generation, it was the other couple that did not fit. Even the canteen lady, even the actors glancing quickly up from their buns and lemonade knew it. For Jason beside his mother was as a new brown conker beside the shell that had once held it. He shone. He carried his head high, he looked at the world with a conqueror's eye. His long grey shorts hung down over his knees, his pullover was loose and khaki-coloured, he wore the uniform of the children of the forties, not of the sleek seventies; but in spite of it, and the cropped head, and the heavy laced up shoes, he vibrated energy, intelligence, life. The little girl, Rebecca, seated at his side on the mock-leather bench, laying her hands tidily upon the moulded white plastic table, looked at him with fear. And his mother knew that she must explain — must get it in before the girl went off to collect the tea — before it all broke open and the inevitable happened again. She caught at the girl's loose sleeve, scanned the surprised calm face, thought that after all, this girl was not such a child, but twenty-eight, perhaps thirty, not a girl but a woman like herself. 'You see,' she said eagerly, 'He was an oxygen-decompression baby. Do you know what that is?'

'Well, vaguely. I read something — about South Africa?'

'Yes, they began it in South Africa. But you can do it here now. We were one of the first. Of course, we had to do it privately, you couldn't get it on the Health. It took all our savings, but then it was worth it. But you see, it's why he's like he is.'

'What?' The girl's face was perplexed, she evidently did not know what the technique was for.

'They get a very high I.Q. It's why he can't keep still. He only sleeps a few hours each night. I can't cope with him. It's too much — and the tears threatened to begin again; she looked down at her trembling hands. Was there something about these statements that did not make sense? The other woman was looking at her as if she was mad. Perhaps she had said something stupid? She thought, now she will leave me, now she will not want to know; for I am about to crack open, this time, I cannot keep the gap closed any longer. And the feeling of water rising, rising about her, began to threaten her again.

But the other woman did not look away or look embarrassed. Puzzled, concerned, yes. But all she said was, 'Look, I'll get the tea, shall I? Then you can tell me.'

'Yes.Yes.'

'No, I know. You get the tea and I'll look after the children. Okay? Surprised, Jason's mother went off, joined the queue, chose cakes and biscuits for the children. She knew what the girl had done in forcing her to go, to pay, to choose. When she came back with the tray, she held her head higher, she saw without the blur of tears. But what she saw amazed her, so that she stopped still, slopped the tea, watched as if she were outside a window. Jason, having stirred all the white and brown sugar together in the two bowls, lifted one up and poured its contents on to the floor; then he looked deliberately across at the other mother, awaiting her reaction. Rebecca watched too, eyes flickering from Jason to her mother and back again, to see what would happen.

'Well, Jason,' said her mother in a clear voice, 'What about the other one? Aren't you going to empty that too?'

Jason looked up, brown eyes bright, lower lip just caught between his teeth, showing his surprise. Tentatively he took the other bowl and tipped a little of the mixed sugar on to the floor. The small group of actors at the next table looked up and grinned and raised their eyebrows, Jason's mother recognised them as the rats from the play; some of them still wore rat-costume from the waist down and curled their tails away behind the legs of chairs.

'Go on, then. There's still some left. Aren't you going to tip it all out?'

Jason looked; saw the amused glances rest casually upon him and move away again; said at last, 'No.'

'Well, then,' said the young woman, 'I can have some in my tea, can't I?' And she smiled at his mother and gratefully took the cup. The children chose their cakes, Rebecca a chocolate eclair, Jason a yellow cup cake. As soon as Rebecca had bitten into hers, Jason snatched it from her and crammed it into his mouth.

'Jason!'

'It's all right,' said Rebecca, reaching for the cup cake, I don't like eclairs, anyway.' And she began carefully to peel away the corrugated paper. Jason, his mouth full, spurting cream, tried to grab the cup cake from her too. But she turned her back on him and went on peeling the paper. 'No,' she said, in a small voice firm with authority, 'You can't have this one, this one's mine.'

Jason, thwarted for the first time that afternoon, let out a roar and grabbed at her hair. Rebecca screamed and pulled away. But at the same moment, one of the actors from the next table sprang up, confronted Jason, legs spread in an exaggerated gun-pulling position, fingers stretched out in imitation of a two-barrelled gun. 'Reach', he said, 'Come on, stick 'em up.' A tall thin man in blue jeans and a tee shirt, with heavy pink make-up still on his face from being one of the councillors of Hamelin town; he lured Jason from his seat, fingers at the child's back, body curved into a menacing slouch. Delighted Jason looked back — at his mother, at the others who would try to confine him — and in a sudden movement whirled, turned upon the man, stuck up his own two fingers in a fury of aggression, shouted, 'I've got you now, mister, keep walking!' The actor groaned and flung away an imaginary gun and put up his hands, mounted the open staircase towards the circle bar with the weary dragging step of a man defeated. Jason marched immediately behind, his fingers prodding the man's back at each hesitation, but was unprepared when the actor pretended to stagger at the fourth step, turned, clutched him, knocked the gun from his hand, tried to hold him down; he nearly fell, and his mother gasped her alarm from below; a horde of men seemed to be coming up the stairs towards him, some dressed as rats, some made up, some named except for jeans. He stood his ground above the body of the man who had collapsed and expired at his feet, he stuck out his chest and stuck out his gun and only as they were a step or two away did he turn and begin to run, across the expanse of floor to the bar, back to where the programme sellers had stood, back again to the head of the staircase. 'Go it, Jason, I'm with you!' shouted one of the young men, and flattened himself against a wall, his two fingers a gun cocked. The chase, the battle grew faster; himself and a couple of others against the whole gang; and he led them, he drew them on, he was intoxicated, committed, alive at last and allowed to be. The theatre bar was empty, the canteen held only a couple of people; there were only the actors and himself and down there, unimportant, his mother and her friend and that silly girl. He could have gone on and on, he was alight with his triumph, but the young men, quickly bored, dropped away to return one by one to their meal of cakes and sandwiches. 'Go it, Jason,' was all they said now, quieter. 'You've won, Jason.' 'That's the lot, kid.' He was alone again. He drooped against the staircase. 'Come on, Jason, and finish your tea,' his mother called out to him, and to the young men she said, 'Thank you ever so much for playing with him.' It was finished.

'His Dad's got so strict with him,' she was saying; and her listener, all sympathy, sprawled across the table beside her with a cigarette in her hand. It was such a relief to tell it all; and yet, who would understand? From the face of the woman who listened, she saw that there was something missing in her story, or something which should not be there. 'He'd beat him,' she said, 'If I was to tell him what happened this afternoon. I have to keep it all to myself. But you can't keep a child in all the time, can you? I mean, if I don't take him out a bit, he'll be like a wild animal when he grows up. I feel I have to keep trying, and maybe one day it'll be all right. I think he needs it, you know, culture, plays and books and things. He'll get to appreciate it, with his I.Q. being what it is. But it does wear me out, I must say, I get so nervous about what he might do. And people aren't always so kind, not like these actors. Mostly it's like what it was this afternoon, with those ladies.'

'But why?' It was the question that had been in the other woman's face, all this time, and she was puzzled by it.

'Why what?'

'Well, why did you do it? The oxygen de-compression thing?'

'Well — ' and she was surprised herself now, that somebody so intelligent, with all the right education, should not have understood. 'Well, it was to give him the best start in life.   The best chance. We all want that for our children, don't we? It was my husband's idea, that we should try it. He's a scientist, you see. I used to go along for these sessions, at a hospital in London it was, where they teach students. The equipment all had to be specially imported. He wanted me to go, you see, it was his idea, but then I was keen too, when I understood what it meant. And when he was born, they got him out by suction. That way, none of the brain cells get damaged. They put a rubber thing over your — you know — during labour, and it sucks. And the baby comes out — pop — like a cork out of a bottle. And she laughed, in spite of herself; it was such a relief to be able to tell somebody about it all. 'And even when he was a tiny baby, he was always that energetic. He was up on his feet at seven months. He's been running around ever since. We did try to get him into a nursery school, and they said he was obviously very bright, but they were afraid they just couldn't cope with him.'

'So you have to.'

'Yes. All the time. My husband won't, he can't stand the way he carries on in public, being so badly behaved. I don't like to leave Jason with him anyway, because I know Jim'll beat him if he misbehaves.'

'Beat him? And it was him who wanted you to do it in the first place,' There was a flaw, she knew it. She said, 'I was thinking of leaving him, you see. I was thinking of getting a divorce.'

'Well, why don't you do it?'

'Well, I have been thinking of it.' She did not, could not understand, not a girl with that sort of energy and confidence; that one could not just do things, because one was sapped of all initiative, exhausted, unable to make a move. To lift one's hands out of one's lap, to clap or boo. It had all been eroded too long ago. But she had made her sacrifice, that she would say, and in spite of it all, Jim, and the students peering up her, and the hot days she spent in that hospital room, wrapped up in plastic, she would do it all again, for Jason.

'But it's your life,' the girl was saying impatiently — and where was Jason now, he was up those stairs again, would be getting into yet more mischief, she must go after him — 'You'll have to do something. You'll just crack up if you go on like this, you can see it a mile off. How old are you, d'you mind my asking.'

'Thirty-four. I was thirty when Jason was born.'

'You're five years older than me. And you look like an old woman. Look, he'll be going to school soon, won't he, and you'll be much freer. It won't last like this. When's he five? And couldn't you get somebody to mind him, just for an hour or so each day, till he goes to school? Surely that wouldn't be impossible. And then you could do something you want to do. Train for something, get out of the house. What did you do before you were married? Christ, you must, you really must. It's your life, after all, isn't it?' The girl spoke with weary impatience, unable to conceal what she felt. But she did not understand; nobody who had not made that choice could understand. She did not see that one day it would all be made even, all repaid to her; when Jason, acclaimed as the genius he would be, would hand her the accolade. The girl was looking at her, frowning, biting a nail, the empty tea cup before her pushed away. One should not tell other people about one's life, Jason's mother thought, for they only started to want to interfere. 'Oh no,' she said quite simply, beginning to put her things away in her bag again, to collect her gloves and her scarf, 'Oh no, you don't understand. It's Jason's.'

Maroons

'Two blue pigeons -
One was black and white — pom!
Sandy he belongs to the mill,
The mill belongs to Sandy still,
Sandy he belongs to the mill
And the mill belongs to Sandy —'

The two of them, ten years old and shouting into the sea wind. Along the sea wall where the waves came and beat at the concrete. Up past the martello tower on the dried mud road where tyre marks cut deep made walking hard. Along the marshes, along the banks of the brown river which was as wide as the sea. 'Two blue pigeons!' A big travelling fair came and settled behind the town, camped upon the dried mud;

at night there was the sudden scream of music in the wind, as the wind moved quarter; all through the long cold summer twilights the crowds wound out there like a long thick serpent nosing home. They went and rode upon the terrifying swing boats, the long-armed machines that hurtled small boxes through the air. Coming home, they wore candy floss upon forehead and nose-tip. Rose felt sick again; it was the year she was always feeling sick. There was too much of everything, too much candy floss. The sky was huge, a vast East Anglian expanse of changing light, beaten by the wind. The land was flat, wider than she had ever seen, and people moved on it as if they did not matter. The houses by the sea wall stood tight together against the sea, and at night the round stones on the beach were pounded against each other until the noise entered one's head. These things did not worry Elizabeth. Elizabeth watched the holiday visitors at the yacht club bar, their neat three-quarter-length jeans, the glamour of their seagoing yellow. She slept soundly at night, in the shared attic room, and never heard the sea battering at reason.

Wherever they walked, they sang in unison. 'And so — I go — to fight the foreign foe —

although — I know I'll be often missed by the girls I've kissed — ' Along the sea wall in the other direction. To the corner shop to buy cigarettes for Elizabeth's mother, twenty Players, once or twice a day. Down to the fish and chip shop in the late half-dark to queue for fish and chips in steaming newspaper when Elizabeth's parents went out for dinner. And they would sit on the sea wall, legs dangling, and bang their sandshoes against the concrete. There was a line of green over the sea and the wet chips tasted of vinegar. A man in a kilt came and walked up and down on the shingle, right at the edge of the sea, and lifted his bagpipes against the sky and played 'Loch Lomond' and 'Speed, Bonny Boat.' The sound filled the whole empty beach, the empty front down as far as the Moot Hall; there was the echo, as when a dog howls.The two girls sat in silence and let the chip papers flutter away and their own legs grow cold. Later, when Rose heard the word 'neglect' she thought of vinegar, the chill sea wind, the movement away from the warm yellow lighted shop; frying tonight, haddock, skate, cod, and the hot packets taken from a greased hand; and the desolation of that sound.

Till ten, till eleven, it was not yet dark over the eastern sea.

'There she is!' A whisper cut short the loud singing; and it was not the bagpipe man this time, but the woman who never turned, never acknowledged them. They began to follow her, by day, by evening; hoping for a full sight of her strange face, a glance from her eyes that might explain her. But she hardly noticed them, or so it seemed. What they saw was her determined back, the head with its crisp curling bush of hair, the deep blue polo collar of her fisherman's sweater — her straight back and legs and buttocks insignificant in worn men's jeans. She wore sea-boots, usually, with the tops turned down. From her belt, rubbing against the blue denim, hung a large pocket knife. It was the knife that Rose loved. And the woman they called 'the Gipsy' strode from her moored boat to the door of the yacht club, swung through it with careless ease and disappeared from their view.

'The one in the trousers with the knife,' Elizabeth's mother made them both sit in the bath and soaped them, one each end, to get the salt off. 'Butch' was the word she used, which they did not know. Rose, shivering under the constant drip of the cold tap at her end, thought of a slab running with blood; a sacrifice, butchered.

'Put your knees down, Rose, love, there's no need to sit all hunched up like that.'

'There isn't room.'

'Soon be needing a bra, won't you? Lucky girl. And not a sign on Elizabeth.' Rose's tears fell unnoticed. Elizabeth's mother stood up, rubbed dry her long white hands with their red nails, spoiled a white towel. She said, 'She's called Margaret Stuart.'

Later, they sat at a round table to eat Weetabix and milk, to make up for the evenings of fish and chips, the neglect. Elizabeth's father, stretched out invisible in his long chair, said, 'I hear Miss Stuart's going to be warned off.'

'What?'

'Well, they don't like it, you know, at the Yacht Club. Women going in and drinking whisky on their own, like that. She uses the place like an old lag.' Lag, butch; the blunt vocabulary of insult.

She sails her boat like a man. That Dragon. 'It's not everybody who could.'

'She does everything like a man, if you ask me.'

Elizabeth's mother laid down a tipped cigarette, stained red at the end. She drew out a little round gold case that contained a cake of pink powder, and the smell was of stale flowers. Automatically she peered and rubbed, admired the final matt effect, snapped the little case shut. Her nails, crimson, snagged at the table cloth. Rose looked beyond to the wild sky over the sea, spooned up a last mouthful, dared the sickness to recur. It appeared, first a tinge, a taste in the mouth, curdling milk; but she fought with it and held it down, saying nothing. Elizabeth in the bedroom asked curiously, 'What is the matter with you, Rose?' But when Rose did not answer, she sighed her acceptance of such strangeness. Going early to bed, they resumed their farting competition of the night before.

She was everywhere, during the week that followed; they had so wanted to see her, and now they found her everywhere. They dawdled outside the yacht club and saw her go in, saw her come out. At the little shop, she was there, buying — not groceries, not cosmetics, — string. A grown woman, buying string. They stood behind her, Elizabeth with the money in her hand for cigarettes and stamps and shoe polish, Rose touching the warm sacks of potatoes that stood in the dark; they could have leaned forward, either of them, touched the knife, said 'good morning', warned her. But they stood aside to let her pass and she went out without seeing them, blindly into the pale sunlight, and the door rang behind her.

'Quick', said Elizabeth, 'We'll drop these in, leave them at the bottom of the stairs, then they won't catch us. If we run, we'll get down in time to watch her launch the boat.'

She bought string, the woman, carefully comparing thicknesses and strengths. She strolled down to sail her boat when she felt like it. She strode through the yacht club bar room, ignoring everybody, ordering whisky. Sometimes she sat alone on bollards, her feet apart, just staring, smoking; and at these times the girls did not dare to come near. She existed, independent of other people's approval; just as, Rose thought, she and Elizabeth existed when they stood in the queue in the fish and chip shop and marched away with their parcels up to the sea wall. It was possible to be an adult woman, and free. One could wear a knife, walk alone, bring coins from the depths of one's trouser pocket to buy string. And Rose knew without saying anything that she would study her, copy her, choose this minute the way to freedom. Watching Elizabeth, as her friend bent that moment to tie a shoelace and straightened, flopping back her hair, Rose thought that for Elizabeth it was probably too late.

'In some foreign region — desert region — I'll be full of grit, I'll die — for the flag — if I must — ' They sang, but grew quieter and at last fell silent as they approached the river bank where the boats were moored. The day was filmy, promising heat, mist hung at knee height. They sat, sharing a bollard, a buttock each, feet spread in imitation, elbows propped upon knees. Margaret Stuart, beginning to bai out, turned and gave them a glance and then turned away. She worked silently; there was only the slosh of the water. The river slapped the sides of the boats, the bank, the quay. Heat began to burn them through their shirts. The girls sat and stared as cats sit, with no declared intention. Rose did not know what Elizabeth thought, Elizabeth did not know what Rose thought. It was impossible to speak, to move. Flies came and buzzed around them and they narrowed their eyes against the sun. At last the bailing was finished and Margaret Stuart sat down in her boat and lit a cigarette, her back turned. In sudden accord, the girls stood up and began to walk away, dragging their shoes in the dust. Neither of them spoke until they were well back into the town again, enclosed by the familiar streets where water was shut out by strong walls and houses had always stood, protected between river and sea.

It was that night that the maroons sounded; out of that heat a storm must have grown unnoticed, while the town slept. Far out at sea it grew, a summer storm. How else could great ships with hundreds of men on board blunder into each other and crack into flame? The maroons went, at two in the morning. In the half dark of a summer night, people rushed out of their houses, coats flung on over pyjamas, to launch the boat. At the Moot Hall, there stood crowds already, like refugees. Rose stood beside her friend, strangely dressed, and shook sleep from her eyes, and felt sick. The sea was white, the town black, faces appeared like moons, shouting; there was a patch of red at sea, flowering like blood upon the water.

'A Belgian tanker.'

'How do you know?'

How did anybody know? Rose, hanging at Elizabeth's father's elbow, found herself swept on in the crowd and suddenly lost. The faces that surrounded her were all strange, all turned towards the lifeboat house; and the boats were coming out, they slid with a grinding noise down the beach, over the stones, the crew in their shining caps and the helpers in flapping clothes heaving from behind. There was a splash and a cheer from all the crowd as the boat slipped from their touch and went straight into the waves. The moon made a path for it, towards that fiery point. The second boat followed, more easily. Suddenly, there was nothing to do but return home. And Rose was lost. She had touched the wood of the first boat as it passed, its hotness had torn at her fingers. There had been a moment of feeling as the boat splashed into the water; there had been that painful unnamed emotion, that was unassimilable, that had no place in her life at all. And then the boat merely growing smaller, driving into the sea; other people, the lifeboatmen, were going out to save the unknown Belgians; Elizabeth's mother, in her fur coat, stood suddenly beside her again to claim her and lead her away. 'Wherever did you get to? We thought we'd lost you for good. What your mother would say, I dread to think.'

'But it was for the maroons', Elizabeth said. The maroons. A rocket breaking open the night, letting even children from their beds.

'We'd better go straight back and have hot drinks and get you two to bed. Good heavens, it's nearly four o'clock.'

Over the sea a pale stripe grew, and the land lightened just slightly. It was the first hint of change, of day.

'What'll we have, Horlicks or Ovaltine?'

'Or hot chocolate?'

'Ovaltine.'

'Chocolate. No, Horlicks.'

'Ovaltine.'

Bickering, forgetting, they allowed themselves to be hurried home.

And the morning seemed to be weighted, passed with an unfamiliar slowness. Their eyes ached, there was heat but no sun; suddenly there was nothing to do.

'Let's go down to the beach.'

'Don't feel like it.'

'Play tennis against the wall?'

'No.' Rose had never in her life known such uncomfortable lethargy.

'If you two can't find anything better to do, you can go down and get me a packet of fags.'

They dragged, not singing. The songs which had been so enchanting — 'Wipe the beer from your ear with your tie-ee' — were now pointless. Elizabeth said, 'You're going on Tuesday, aren't you?'

Rose nodded, knew that there was still something else, that some ill thing was promised, that this was not to be the end.

'Didn't you know?' The grocer behind the counter stretched to hook down some throat pastilles from a high shelf, talked over his shoulder to the woman who fingered her money. 'I suppose there was so much going on last night, with one thing and another and the boats going out, nobody would have noticed. Tragic thing, really.'

'Where did it happen?' The fat woman just in front of them looked down at her list, only to hide her curiosity.

'Up by the bend in the river. Where the buoys are, for the Round the Island race. That's where they found her, anyway. Odd place to be at night. Easy enough for a boat to turn over there, specially if there was a touch of wind.'

'But she was a good sailor.'

'Miss Stuart? Sailed that boat like a man.'

Silent, together, they left the shop, Elizabeth still holding the money for the cigarettes. What happened? They wanted to ask, but children did not ask, did not intrude. They had to wait, hang about like stray cats waiting to pick up scraps. Everybody was talking about it, now; it was the latest news, newer than the Belgians; they hung about and waited, and at last heard it all. Miss Stuart, sailing alone at night, had overturned her boat on the sharp bend of the river, and drowned. She had been found. Rose saw her, the curly hair spread like weed, the knife in its soaked sheath; like a hero, upon a bier. She was dead, and people believed that she had deserved it. Everybody had come out of their houses and cheered to see the lifeboat go out to save those Belgians, and Miss Stuart, all alone, had simply drowned. Rose had stood and touched the wood of the lifeboat with something like a prayer going through her mind; she had stood as women had stood for centuries upon the shore, watching the men go out.

'She must have been a lonely soul, in a way' was one of the epitaphs they heard, that morning, in the shops of the small holiday town, that last holiday morning of a summer in the early nineteen-fifties. It was the one which Rose remembered, and which she did not want to believe.

Tuesday came. Along the station platform they marched, Rose in her shoes and socks and clothes for going home. Elizabeth's mother bought a ticket, stacked cases upon the hot peeled bench. Along the platform they went, the two of them, striding in time. Elizabeth suddenly friendly, seeing her go. And sang, as they had once sung all the way along the beach, out to the yacht club, along the sea wall, in those days before the maroons went up. It was not the same, now, but they tried. Sang. Rose with the knowledge of something that flowed out of her, that would always flow out of her now. Goodbye-ee, don't cry-ee, wipe the beer from you ear with your tie-ee, though it's hard to part I know, I'll-be-tickled-to-death to go, so goodbye-ee. . . . .

Lemmings

The restaurant was empty; forty places laid for diners, knives and forks geometrical, each white cloth stiff and clean, standing out slightly from the table. One walked across the floor, on soft carpet, between tables; one was conscious of being watched, of having to be perfect. Slipped on to the chair, let a shawl slide back, looked around one, picked up a menu, played with a glass. An expensive place. A treat. But why so empty? And at the end of the evening, all this whiteness would be stained with sauce and wine. One was silent, because there might be an echo. Here, one was escorted, one was passive. But they would have a good laundry, a careful service, pure white would be restored, for the next evening and then again for the next. White for the ritual of despoiling, white for the nothingness of virginity, the uneventfulness of death; white, the paper yet unwritten on, the sheets unmarked with sex. And this white was already the past. One crumbled bread, dropped cigarette ash, crumpled the napkin while putting it on one's lap. Could we have some water, please? One asked, and things were brought. This situation was already the past, so that one was no longer easy in it, no longer at ease. This will have to change, she thought. We are the last people in the world. The last ones who can choose, who can pay. Will it be our blood that marks the tablecloth?

Other people came, yes, and filled corners quietly, occupied the furthest tables in the room as if they too wanted to hide. There was a movement to and fro, an uncorking of bottles. Her husband waited, eyeing the ice bucket in which his chosen bottle stood. His broad hairy hands holding the menu, still holding it. The unexpected was for him no pleasure; he would have preferred a set meal. She knew so well his pain in having to choose, in fearing. He liked to plan and control, could only enjoy anticipation of the certain future. A fastidious man. Was that true? Look at his hands, at his chin. Arrogance to conceal fear; preferring the known thing. But giving her a treat, giving her this restaurant, this menu, this unknown. Looking at him, she saw him suddenly as she knew him otherwise; eyes dilated in sudden fear as his sperm rushed out of him and into her, as he cried out as any other man might at that moment. The waiter was there, wanting their decision. Howard looked up from the menu, past his wife's eyes. He said with unusual firmness, 'I'll have the dover sole, and the prawn cocktail to begin with.' He had not asked her what she would have. Perhaps he had forgotten?

She said, looking up at the waiter, 'I'll have the same.' It annoyed her, to want what he had already chosen, yet she helplessly wanted it all the same. To think of it, juices flowed into her mouth.

She said, 'You had haddock for breakfast.'

'So did you.'

'No, I only had toast.' She had wondered if she might at last be pregnant again. He had wanted it so. And now, with this longing for fish, this taste in her mouth, this craving, she wondered.

At breakfast, not wanting him to ask, she had left him all the smoked haddock and eaten only toast. 'Have a good lunch?' He had eaten in a pub, she supposed, and only asked her out of politeness. 'You ought to have a good lunch, if you only have toast at breakfast. I don't think you eat properly, on your own.'

'Oh, yes. Quite good. I wasn't terribly hungry, I just had some cheese and fruit,' she lied to him.

'You don't think ...?'

'Oh no, I'm sure not. No, I couldn't be, really.' She laughed; and there was the unkind echo in the too-big room. But in her mind there appeared like a small growing spot the resolve to tell him, so that everything would be fair and open between them on this tenth anniversary of their marriage. Yet she could not tell him; he would laugh at her if she told him now; how she had gone out at lunch time and bought half a pound of smoked salmon and eaten it all herself without even a squirt of lemon, behind closed doors.

'Where did you go?' She looked down; knew that he knew he was deceived.

'Oh, the usual. The George. They do some quite good sandwiches.'

'What sort of sandwiches?'

'Oh, I don't know, ham, prawn, cheese and chutney.'

'And you had prawn?'

'No,' he said, 'No, I didn't. Actually I had cheese, cheese and chutney.' She smiled at his lie, at his slight blush. Years ago, they had promised each other that if either of them should want to take a lover, the other should feel free to do so, that if one were to embark on a secret life, the other might make up the balance. She would hold on to her smoked salmon now.

The food came, and they began to eat in silence, each digging deep into the mounds of prawns and mayonnaise, each scraping up the juice from the little glass cup, each finally mopping up the very last tastes with their bread. They were absorbed, not speaking; as if at work.

Howard said, looking at her uncertainly, 'D'you think we might perhaps have the same again? After all, we are celebrating. It isn't every day.'

Helen looked at him. For a moment their glance lingered, as if love had returned; and then she found the self-punishment within her that was her only way to mortify him, and said,

'What, another prawn cocktail? When we have sole to follow?' After all, he had almost certainly lied to her about his lunch.

'No, I suppose not.' His fingers drummed the table in frustration, but he would not give way, not admit to her, not yet. 'Will you have some more wine, dear?' he asked her. They watched the clear pale liquid rise up the glass. When they drank, they found it a little too sweet, a little too strong, somehow not quite satisfying. Howard's face moved as if he had swallowed medicine; he waved to the waiter and Helen thought he was going to send the wine back, to say that it was corked, bad, anyway not what they wanted.

'Could you bring us some salt, please?'

'But there is salt, sir, on the table.' A small cruet, the salt pot with the top screwed off.

'We've finished it.'

'Oh, yes. Sorry, sir, we must have forgotten to fill it. One moment, and I'll bring you some more. Was the wine all right, sir?'

'Sea salt', Howard said, 'If you've got it. Quite a lot, we shall need.'

'A lot. Er, yes, well, I'll see if we have some. Did you find the wine all right, sir?'

When the bowl came, Howard sat dipping wet bread into the heap of flaky off-white crystals and eating it. His eyes, as he ate, were fixed on something beyond her, so that she wondered if, while they had been eating, another woman had sat down at the table beyond them; but, turning, she saw nobody. Only the object of his attention, a picture hanging on the wall, an ordinary bad painting of a seaside place somewhere in Italy, with boats and gulls. It was then that she began to feel pain; as if an old abscess in a tooth had been touched, pain that began somewhere precise but that spread all through her, to fill even her fingers and toes with the agony of something lost, something amputated. She stretched her mind and her senses to try to find out what it was. She must be able to remember. She sniffed, licked her lips, moved her painful extremities and turned her head this way and that like a hound to find the scent; and caught her husband's eye. Without speaking, he pushed the dish of salt towards her. Like him, she began to eat it, and as if it were a drug, the pain eased and the acute discomfort, the tension, began to die away.

She said after a moment, 'Howard, have we been poisoned? Are we ill? But before he could answer, the plates of fish arrived, and each of them began to bite them up, snapping the small bones in their teeth.

That night was one of the worst that she could remember. It was August, and the day's heat had not faded but rather intensified during the evening. Coming out of the cooled restaurant had been like getting into a warm bath. Now she lay beside Howard but apart from him and knew from his sighing and turning that he too was awake. 'Howard? Howard?' She said it once again, quietly, as if to experiment. But he did not answer and only turned again, away from her. Her waking dreams and his were the same, incommunicable; and together they lay for the whole short summer night, apart, not touching, involved in the same torment. The idea of poison returned to Helen; but what poison, how, and from where? She was infected, she was cursed with a sense of not being whole, of being only partial. The feeling was close to strong sexual desire; yet it was not her husband, not any man whom she wanted, and her mouth, rather than her genitals, seemed to be open and gasping, dried up, longing to be filled. A smell, a strong smell seemed to be somewhere just beyond her reach, a smell she longed for as one would long for the body smell of an absent lover. Seaweed. Was that it? Yes, seaweed, strong, rank, slimy under bare feet, rotting in the sun, drifting in great wads, on the tide, to and fro, to and fro. The smell. And the brush of weed, like hair in the cool depths, the gliding, darting of fish in the darkness of the sea's cellars. Numbness, cold, relief. She sat up, pushing back the damp sheet from her naked body; but there was nothing, nothing she could do. She drank water from the bathroom tap, spattering her face and neck and breasts with drops. She lit a cigarette and stood for a moment puffing at it, feeling a slight cool touch from the window, air upon the wetted parts of herself. She touched her body, fingered herself a little, as if surprised at her own changing sensations. It was as if her skin were raw, as if she were terribly sunburned, and helplessly now exposed to the touch of air. When she got back into bed, even the sheets hurt her. If she moved, the itching began again, that grew up her legs and back and into her scalp. Impetigo, she thought, chickenpox, scurvy, shingles. A nervous disease, an allergy. That must be it. Allergy. But to what? She would see the doctor, and in the morning be reassured.

She slept for perhaps an hour. Towards dawn, Howard got out of bed, and she woke painfully to hear him pad towards the kitchen on bare feet and open and shut cupboard doors. As if searching, and determined to find. When he came back, outlined in the grey dusky light, she saw that he was carrying something, holding it out to her. A tin of sardines? Together, in silence, they picked out the fish with their fingers and licked up the oil and crunched up the backbones in their teeth. When they had finished, he looked at her, his face clearer now in the rising light, and it was as if they had made love, as if this time they were really together. Curled close, the empty tin on the floor beside them, their oily hands upon each other, they slept for an hour or so.

There was a narrow strip of lawn and a fence and two neat paths and some rose beds, between the two houses. In an identical house to their neighbours, John and Abigail Shelton were quarrelling. Already the dawn light made a white square beyond the windows and there were the first sounds of a beginning day.

John said, 'It's hardly surprising, if you must guzzle all that lobster at dinner, you can hardly be surprised if you get indigestion. Why don't you take an Alka-Seltzer? I didn't know where to look, with you taking so much, I mean, people don't ask you out to share a lobster to have you eat the whole thing. Nobody else got a look-in. I was really embarrassed. I don't know what came over you. Now for God's sake go and take something, and then can we please get some sleep. I've got to get to work in the morning somehow.'

'You haven't, it's the holidays. Check. And it isn't indigestion.'

'Oh, yes. Well, whatever it is, shut up, Abby, go to sleep.'

She sat up in bed, just as Helen Peel next door had sat up, and stared round the room which they had disguised with books and clothes and tacked-up pictures. The clean empty spaces of the Peels' bedroom became the cluttered floor of the Sheltons'. Abigail's nightdress slipped from her shoulders and her dark hair fell about her. She wanted him to wake up now, so that they could make love. But she said, loud, 'Just because you're so fussy about your stomach. Anyway, I didn't have all that much, so don't be so unfair. And it's just that I can't stand it any more, that's all.'

'What?' he growled from the pillow, flung out an arm to grope for a cool empty place.

'This place. It's getting me down. It makes me feel — I don't know — dead. And you never used to be so bourgeois, going on about Alka-Seltzer all the time and watching how much I eat. It just erodes you, that's all, bit by bit. You have to know when to stop. When to say no.'

He said, 'That's just what I was saying about your greedy performance tonight. And anyway, Alka Seltzer's only alkali to counteract the acid you pour down you, it doesn't erode the stomach like aspirin. Oh, do go to sleep, for heaven's sake, I'm exhausted.'

'I don't mean bloody Alka-Seltzer', she shouted, 'I mean this house, this place, this town, the claustrophobia, the sameness, all the people, this ghastly heat, the dirt everywhere. Don't you feel it? Don't you feel you're gradually being eaten away?'

He sighed, renouncing sleep. His voice slow, level, he said, 'Well, where d'you want to go?, that isn't claustrophobic, dirty, bourgeois hot and eating you away? Just decide that, and then perhaps we can get some sleep.'

'Somewhere quiet. Somewhere cool, with water.'

'The sea.'

'The sea. Not the Mediterranean. A cold clean northern sea. I can just see it. Empty beaches, and the wind.'

'I thought we'd decided on skiing at Christmas. I thought we'd agreed on that. Austria, with the kids. You can't have it both ways.'

'We can afford it.'

'What?'

'The sea. Can't we? I do hate towns in hot weather. It would do you so much good. And the children are bored stiff, with all their friends away.'

'What about the Peel children? They're here.'

'Oh, the Peels, yes', she said, 'But what about me? I think I will get myself an Alka-Seltzer after all.'

At breakfast, while she stirred coffee in the jug and looked for some clean cups, he came in unshaven in his dressing gown, barefoot on the Marley tiles. 'Abby, you haven't got any kippers, have you, anything like that? I just woke up thinking I could fancy a kipper.'

'Kippers?' She looked at him strangely, as if divining water.

'Yes, kippers, I said kippers. Or haddock, even.'

'You don't usually eat a cooked breakfast.'

'Hell, I know I don't. But I just thought, today.'

'Actually, I have got some kippers. Look.'

She brought them out of the fridge and laid the paper open on the table and sniffed their tarry strength.

'Six?' He stared at her.

'Well, we could have three each. Put the pan on, John, we'll eat them before the children come down.' He moved as if dazed, still; and when they looked at each other it was with wariness and embarrassment. They sat down opposite each other with the morning sun flooding the floor at their feet, and began to eat. Neither of them stopped to pick out the bones. The juicy fawn meat was thick between their teeth, and there was more, yet more of it to eat. Abigail laughed and said, 'This is a bit like being an alcoholic, know what I mean? I feel as if we're going on a bender.' He recognised the slight tilt of hysteria in her voice, and put out a hand. His breath was fishy, close to her. He licked the oily drops from his lips and rubbed his hand across his mouth; and in a moment she had seized his fingers and was licking each separate one. The cat sat between them, the tabby tom with his bent right ear; he sucked in his breath and from his throat came a little croak of longing.

'Mummy. I can smell fish.' Thomas swung the door open and stood there, cotton pyjamas open upon his small tanned belly, the trousers sagging around his feet. He watched them at the end of their feast. His mother crammed in a last mouthful and gabbled at him, 'There are eggs for you, Tom, nice fried eggs. We were saving the eggs for you and Janie. Daddy and I were just — finishing up a few old kippers we found.'

'I want kippers.'

'Kippers,' the little girl echoed, four years old and always just standing behind him, her mouth trembling, ready for tears. A mobile face, prepared in life for grief.

'Nice eggs. Now go and get dressed, darlings and I'll get your corn flakes and eggs.'

'We want kippers!' They moved away, grumbling. Unbelieving, to see their mother eat the last mouthful before their eyes, and their father replete and silent, and the cat crouched to move in, licking the plates as he had never been allowed to do before.

Again, there was the long drawn-out heat of the August day. The city streets made of dust and burning tar, the parks deserts of white grass. Railings like hot pokers, and the seats of children's swings too hot even to touch through cloth. In the suburbs there was a slight wind, but hot, smelling metallic, as if blown from a hair-dryer. And after the early morning, no shade anywhere, no cooling place. Milk was warm already upon doorsteps. The walls still held yesterday's heat. In the choked roads, between the buildings, car engines turned over and petrol fumes invisibly filled the air. Soon there would be nothing left to breathe, no way of facing the harsh light. And the city, itself brittle as an engine tried too far with heat, shook as if it would fall apart. It shook, and shed grit and dust. And everywhere, right out to the grassier suburbs where the Peels and the Sheltons lived, there spread the taste and smell of its putrefaction. It was a freak year, everyone said. It was never this hot in England. As if it had no right to be, as if in saying this, it might be reversed. And there was a kind of panic, a kind of fear in the air. People talked of escape, instead of holidays; of 'getting away' and 'getting out of here'; as if the place itself, as if the air were a prison. It can't go on like this, they said. It will have to stop. We will simply have to get away. Are you getting away this year? Will you be able to escape?

Helen Peel stood in the queue outside the fish shop and was surprised to see how many people whom she knew were there. The fishmonger was sweating, patting his head with a handkerchief, swishing flies off the cod steaks. He had run right out of prawns and kippers, he said, and of haddock too. There was cod, or a nice bit of halibut. Would that do? Of course, it was getting pricey, but it was on account of the sudden demand. Helen paid nearly a pound for her piece of halibut. There were two women, one of them a magistrate, fighting over the last crab. She saw Abigail Shelton with one of her grubby children who was crying for fish paste; and the last pot of bloater had just gone. She heard Abigail soothe the child, 'Never mind, Tom, we'll go home and I'll make you a nice drink of salt water, and we have still got some sardines left, I promise.' Something was happening. She stood alone in the street and felt the sun strike the top of her head through her headscarf, she felt its brutality, its attack; — she saw the queues, the cars, the harassed people; and she knew, something was happening now that had not happened before, that was peculiar to this time, her life, this moment in the whole of existence. Suddenly, she was very much afraid.

They left the cars parked on a strip of tarmac, and walked together, the little group of them, between the bents and marram grass, their feet sinking into the soft sand. The breeze started just gently and came to them from the sea, dusting their faces with salt. Their hair moved, their skin became alive with it, they quickened their pace, and holding the children's hands, began even to run downhill, from the sandhills down to the harder damper sand at the sea's edge. It was a low tide; there would be a long way to go. But it must have turned, just now, John said, it must be beginning to come in. It would cover all footprints, all traces. He took off his sandals and stamped in the wet seaweed. One of the children, Tom, began to roll like a puppy, till he was soaked and smeared with sand, weed in his hair and upon his cheek. The others followed, rolling, shouting. The little waves greeted them at the edge of the sea. They were warm, they were familiar. They moved around the angles; deeper, they swelled up against the thigh. Helen took Howard's hand and he clasped hers hard as they waded in. She thought of that moment before her confirmation; suddenly, that long ago moment, when she was nearly fourteen, before she had realised that the bishop's touch upon her head would work no miracle. With her free hand, she held her daughter Tamsin to her, close to the solemnity of the moment that passed, that moment of absolute belief, in which she was free, relieved of doubt and responsibility. They had waded on calmly, as if this were a ford, a way out to something else; the long line of people striding into the sea. Water dragged at their feet, making them slow. Now there was the deep water before them, around them. The sea, its face dark, light, smooth, rippled, as changing and various as the human mind. Behind them they had left the land, the old land; impoverished, scrawled upon, overused, the cities that rotted, the places in which they saw no reflections. They could stand still, now, and watch the sea move. The strong wafting smells filled them; water and weed and fish. Some of them were in the water already, now, turning and wallowing like porpoises; others still hesitant, held back.

Howard Peel said to John Shelton, across the frolicking children, 'Is this it?' Are you sure? Or could we still go back and live there?'

He received no answer, for John was underwater, surfacing, water streaming from his hair and yes, a man all fluid and slippery now, beyond reach. 'Wait!' Howard shouted, 'Wait! Just a minute!' to the others he glimpsed behind him, to the advancing lines of people who were following him into the sea. But his cry was lost, it was a mute gasp, it was carried away from him; it was already too late; he was falling, he was colliding with something heavy, sinking, fighting; a blackness in his eyes and a congestion in his lungs, as he struggled, as he hunted for the thought that had flown out with his last human breath, as he groped in his mind for his last construction as a man. It came to him, as he surfaced for the third time, as he glimpsed air and light for the last time. The question. The question he wanted to shout, but his mouth was filled with salt water: 'Then have we gills? If this is our evolution, have we gills?' And as the sea easily claimed him with the others, the vision in his fading man's mind was of a fish he had once caught, that had reeled and gasped and twisted on the bone-dry boards of his boat, and found the air failing, and died.

Afterwards, the sea in its blank purity showed no trace.

Revolution

Up at the Hall, they were all on parade. The flowers, the hats, even the women selling teas. There was a parting of May cloud just at the moment of the opening, when Mrs. Bartholomew started selling tickets and the first cars rolled gently over the gravel and the squire himself stepped out through the french windows and padded across his lawn. The sky was patched, deep-blue and white. People argued, which was spreading, the blue or the white. When the sun shone it seemed to go right through and warm the bone; and then again it was gone. Herbert Gibson had been predicting weather all day; he said, watch the vanecock on the church, it'll turn by dinnertime and there'll be a grand afternoon; the moon, he said, came in dry. People quoted him. He was why they did not bring mackintoshes. He was the reason for the summer prints, flowered, the plastic platform sandals that stamped upon the grass; he and the longing for high summer. He stood by the gate and peered at the golden bird that sailed round high on the church spire, and rubbed his hands. Mrs. Bartholomew had brought her plastic hat; it was folded up small, tied with ribbons, beside the unfurling rolls of tickets. Yet she said, smiling, to each one who passed, 'Lovely day, isn't it?' For there was always a good day for the squire's opening; the squire walked in thin shoes and a pale summer suit, proving it. He teetered from his toes to his heels, hands behind his back, and looked over people's heads. His wife rushed about wearing a turquoise coat; greeting people, unaristocratic. I looked at the squire and wondered; and a car came between us, the long cream body of a Bentley. Only the Bentleys and Rolls' came up the drive. It was like a funeral. The others all parked in the field opposite, where the cows usually were, with a notice saying At The Owners' Risk. After the rain, their wheels turned round uselessly in the mud. People left

144

them and came to the driveway and bought their tickets from Mrs. Bartholomew and walked between the yew trees quietly, close together, as if they were in church. I saw children pulled to heel, like little dogs. And the set step of humble feet.

The first time I had been up to the Hall was at the meet, in February; and it was the last time, too. When there was a wind coming at you from round every corner of that foursquare house, on a mean February day. People clustered, then. The squire's wife, warmly tweeded, clutched her handbag. There were servants, blue-fingered, with drinks on trays. A glass of port for everyone, all of us standing in our wellingtons and our too-thin coats, while the warm breath of horses went over our heads. We turned our backs to the wind and stamped our feet a bit and chatted to each other, of colds and schools and children's habits. The doors of the hall stood open, central heating pouring into the air; ancestors looking when you went for a second glass. Miss Pettit stood by the table, pretending to look at pictures, so that her glass was in the butler's way. A man ran in, red-cheeked and blond, shouting for his damn whip. I remembered that glassy light, that cold, those febrile legs of high bred horses trembling on the gravel. There were women then with muzzles pointing into the wind beneath their tiny veils, scenting. Their hands gathering in their horses; capable in that moment of love. And the men were like cord, like leather. They were tuned to a pitch. Their thin thighs upon soft saddle leather, upon flesh. Upon veins, upon velvet. Blood visible beneath their horses' skins. Men and horses motionless, unperturbed by the cut of the wind. Set apart. We did not speak to them nor they to us, we saw them poised there for a moment and then in sudden movement, away across the grass, through the gate, into the far field; a sudden flow. Then we were left, putting back empty glasses, grateful, quiet. And the men with the giant half-timbered horse boxes drove them away, with the second horse in the back waiting for half time; only a nervous gleam of an eye in the dark. They would wait across the country for the first yelp, the first sound of hoofs on tarmac; the men reading folded newspapers among tail-bandages and curry combs, smoking cigarettes, the horses listening, trembling, stamping in the back. Yes.

There was still that chill light upon the front of the house, where nothing grew. The grass so perfect that the shadows of clouds passed over it as if on calm water. The tulips, by the drive, red and yellow, like beads. Surfaces harder, somehow, than outside; objects more distinct. Here, even people one knew well looked odd, delineated. Ordinary people were like people in cartoons. Only the ones who lived here matched. I remembered hearing, at the hunt, 'Of course, it's not the same, not since the Prince of Wales ....' Now we pay, we look, we have the right to observe; but we look absurd, our clothes wrong, accents, movements out of place. I see the squire's wife, trying. She was not born to it. Here, you can see that in a minute. There is no escape. She goes to see if the tea ladies with their urns are well. There are orange cups of tea, little cakes for everyone. We may walk between the tulips, look in at the rooms even through the limpid glass of the tall windows. We may stroll upon the gravel, pretending. Or drop ice cream paper and scream. There are women with pushchairs, with babies in pink and white and husbands in collars and children with stiff, garish dresses, and their feet strut un-comfortably upon high heels and their flesh is all squashed into Sunday clothes; they have come out from the city, paid to come, to look; and in every movement there is such anxiety, that they might drop something, mark something, their children misbehave. Gary, come off that grass. Sharon if you aren't a good girl we'll go back home. Michelle, if you do that once again you'll get a smack. The children bounce and fret among the herbaceous borders, and their fingers long to tweak and pull. Their mothers wonder why they came, why they brought them. This garden is a strain. There is nowhere to hide; sit down; take off one's shoes. The tulips and the roses watch like sentinels. But then they turn a corner and come into the long, shaded walk that leads to the orchards. Here, you can relax; there are pine needles underfoot and dark bushes and the children can run ahead. There is even a dog, panting at the end of a lead, sniffing at the underbrush. It is a blind man's dog; a golden retriever quickly aged with responsibility, its eyes and nose dry. It tugs him on with its strong shoulders, towards the gleam of sunlight at the end of the path. There is the orchard; apple trees and daffodils and long grass, a reward, a gesture; a touch of ease; a reckless English thing. The wind comes and makes the daffodils leap and sway; it is all like a musical box, wound up. People stand still in delight and watch, the performance of May wind and quick, glancing sun, and then go on.

But the music is real. The music comes from under the great tree at the edge of the rose garden, and it is mixed with the jingling of bells. It jigs as the daffodils, the apple branches jig. The Morris men are here. And the accordion sound, as it tunes up and the men begin to shake the bells upon their calves and dance a little, up and down, with their handkerchiefs in the breeze, draws everybody back from the orchard, up from the gravel drive, out of the warmth of the greenhouses where a million tomatoes will ripen and a thousand carnations bloom. People come out and gather together in little groups to watch, as they watched the hunters go out on that winter day. But they are not so careful today; there is no need to worry about putting the port glasses properly back upon the tray, or about not making a thoroughbred horse jump, or about saying the right thing. For the Morris men are just young men from Nottingham. They drink beer out of cans and stub out cigarettes as they start. Their forearms, beneath the rolled back sleeves, are tough with work; and as they dance, they sweat and their skins gleam. The leader is a man with a big stomach that bounces before him. He announces 'from the village of Headington, in Oxfordshire....' and takes the accordion to his belly, his right foot stumping on the ground. Two of the dancers have long hair and it bounces on their shoulders and flies about their eyes. One is bearded, balding. One is small and very red in the face. The shoes that dance are scuffed, worn, and on the clean white shirts patches of sweat begin to appear. In between dances, the men's heads bow, they pant in a controlled way. And staves come out, and they dance and beat at each other, and fight with the crack-crack of wood, like outlaws. Their faces work, their teeth appear in an unconscious smile of effort and pleasure. They have done this often; it is a game, a rite. And in between dances, the people on the lawns, between the rosebushes, grouped on the gravel, applaud quietly and wait for more. The bearded man goes round with a cap and bows with mock servility for coins. The children come forward and drop coins in, and men fish about in their pockets. I half-turn and see the squire standing alone at this point, among the rose bushes, beside the sundial, his glasses caught by the sun. It is the last dance, now. The staves, some of them split from the banging, are dropped on one side. The accordion is put on the bench beneath the great walnut tree, and the man picks up a fiddle, to begin a flippant tune. The dance this time is light and gay; the men's smiles easy; the feet trip and pas-de-bas, and skip and stamp in time. This time, it is as if they are making fun of themselves; it is a lighthearted pastiche. And the man in the fool's cap runs out and swipes at the crowd with his balloon on a stick, and some of the children shriek. The walnut tree's branches lift and sway. A cloud passes suddenly over the sun, darkening the garden. The dance is ending, the dancers in a long chain move sideways, holding hands, capering, waving their farewell. They move towards the squire, where he stands alone, they circle him, they dance a ring-a-roses all around him, their feet exaggerating now, like children; and there he is, an embarrassed middle-aged man at the centre, smiling now at what he takes for homage. In the scattered grounds, in the gardens, a little 'ah' of appreciation goes out; they are thanking the squire, showing everyone's appreciation; how nice, just what was needed, a fitting ending, and now we can go home. But in the 'ah' and the 'how nice' is there just a tremor of something else? Of

151

anxiety, of fear even? That this might all go too far? I cannot be sure. I am watching the squire's face, which is pink and suddenly harassed; he has had enough, he wants to escape now, to laugh a little indulgently, acknowledging thanks for his generosity, and then move away. He is tired, perhaps, of his open day; wants these strangers, all of them, to go; wants to go into his great house as his ancestors have done, and shut the mob out. He looks suddenly frail, suddenly frightened. But it all happens so fast: I see his form appear and disappear again, hidden by the whirl of the dancers. Atishoo! Atishoo! We all fall down! The Morris men are dancing him towards the edge of his own wood, beyond which is the orchard, and then the road. He is being danced to the very edge of his own domain, back to the other world, the road and beyond, where nothing is sacred. I see, feel the gasp and movement of the crowd, but nothing happens. People stare, but cannot move to free him. It has all gone on for too long. The big house, the lawns, the ancient trees, the rosebeds make this impossible. We all of us only gasp and stare and cannot believe our eyes. The figures twirl, small, at the edge of the wood. They disappear. The dancing white men with their bells and the tottering, tall pink-faced squire. We none of us ever saw him again. I suppose you could say it was the end of an era.

The World's End

Initially and throughout, what one finds hardest to bear is the thought of personal extinction. Oh, yes, one has thought about death. It is the salt of our waking life, the small thought that occurs before rising, before sleep. But death sometime, death one day, death when I am old. Now they tell us that it will probably be August 25th. or thereabouts, the death of the world. On that day I and the world will cease to exist. Yes, and it is the thought of the death of all the others that intensifies that of my own. Why should I care, after I am dead, if the world goes on? If I am unable to see it? Because the death of the individual has been at the end always, throughout time. We live with our individual deaths, from the moment of first consciousness. The death of the entire species is something new. Phylogeny here follows ontogeny. My death is the prototype; the rest will follow.

The first clue we had was when he went for an interview, for a job, a job he wanted in another university. In science faculties, they tend to know what is happening first, they tend to keep the truth from other people for as long as they can. Or was it a directive from the government? Jem came home looking puzzled; how could one teach students psychology without reference to the future, using concepts that are only relevant to the present? He asks me. I say, how much present? Until perhaps the autumn, until the beginning of the academic year. What would have been the academic year. I say, how can one do anything without reference to a future, to a possibility not yet realised? I drive along a high country road, talking to him in my mind, fetching our child from school. The day is windy, cold, a day in early spring; light scatters from between the clouds; the new fat grass blades are glossy in occasional sun. Before me a flock of sheep appears from a field gate and I slow right down to let them fill the road and trot to their new destination, the next field down. All around me they jerk along with their stiff-legged rolling gait, the sheep and the growing lambs, in identical movement; back feet to front feet and back again like rocking-horses. The thick wool on each back would bury my whole hand in its oiliness. The ewes run very concentratedly, fixing their little yellow eyes upon the road; and the lambs no longer gambol or play but run fixedly beside their mothers, suddenly adult with my engine behind them; they never turn their black faces and clatter, clatter go their tiny feet. I think, what is the point of lambs, of this year's lambs? There is nothing we can do without an implied future. It is there, implanted in the seed: embryo, foetus, lamb, sheep, carcase. Why do I drive my car along this road, between illusory fields of green that stretch away in the sparse sunlight, under an illusory sky of cloud and darting light and sudden patch of blue?

As the time comes nearer, I begin to keep a diary, in order to make sure that I do something each day. I force myself to think that there will be no posterity, no eye from another century reading on. But nothing in my life has been done because of its value in the present, and how am

I to change now?: school ensured university, girlhood ensured womanhood, my talents and resolutions ensured my qualification as a doctor; love, in my case, ensured marriage and sex, in my case, ensured children. Again, giving birth ensured the slow separate development of another human being. Nothing has interrupted me, in my life. I have often thought guiltily, that I was born to succeed. Now I do a locum and a birth control clinic once a week, in order to ensure that people do not get diseases, in order to ensure that people who do not want babies may live their lives without them and that those who want them in four years' time shall have them then and not before. I have never really been thwarted. No miscarriages, like my sister Jean, no failed exams, no ambitions lasting unsatisfied. Yes, I know I have been lucky.

Now I shall die at thirty-two.

Family life is constructed around a belief in the future, we have children, we expect them to grow up, to have their children, we expect to grow older together, to develop new interests, to have more free time. Jem and I do, although this is not the fashion. Jem takes the new job which has been offered to him, the chair of behavioural psychology at the new university;

he is not yet forty; he too has become accustomed to success. When we make love now, in the early summer, as the nights grow warmer, the evenings longer and lighter, I hear myself think: what is the point? And neither is there any point in talking about it much more, the thing which is coming. We could go on holiday, we could travel to see the world; take the children out of school, give up work, burn up our money in the time that is left. All around us, people are going off on cruises; to the Andes, Jamaica, India, the Pole. But those who are used to work find it easier to go on working; and we move still with continuity in our blood.

Alan Halliday drops in one evening; he is hiring a horse, a ride across Hungary; it is what he has always wanted to do. Jem tells me that Danny and Catherine are going to cross the Atlantic in a plastic boat. They will just have time to get to the other side. Adam says to me, hanging around the kitchen door, 'Why can't I leave school? Jim Parkinson's leaving, he's going round the world.' Jem tells him, 'The world is round, Adam, when you go round it you come back to the very point at which you started.' And Adam kicks at the skirting board, 'You are stupid, Dad, I know that, that's not the point.' The point is, Jem says, to go on doing useful work. He makes jokes: Apocalypse Tours; round Armageddon and back. None of us has really been able to believe it.

There is a mark in my diary, a mark made upon the year. When it will begin, the end. And now the newspapers, the television concentrate on this point almost exclusively, so that the mark is everywhere, in diaries, calendars, minds, faces. I am reminded of the time, some years ago, when we all changed over to decimal currency because a government had decided we would; how until the day — D-day, it was called — nobody could quite believe that it was possible, that the ancient penny, the shilling, would be no more. But the clocks went on, the day came and went, and the new money was with us and everybody started using it, just as they were told to. Again, it happened when the new legislation came in about birth control, turning my clinic upside down; nobody could quite believe that contraception was no longer the haphazard thing of the past. Now there is something else that we must get used to: imminent destruction. They are preparing us for it well. Preachers of various denominations have taken over all the channels. God is everywhere. They come to our door, children in faded denims and black clothes, telling us that after death we will be saved. There is room in heaven for thousands, millions, for the whole erring destructive world. Never have I seen such a religious revival. There still exist small protesting letters from humanists and atheists; there still exist myself, Jem, our calm rationalist minds with which we grew up, which now cannot be changed.

We will be able to watch the beginnings of it on television. It will be like a moon-landing in reverse, the proof of man's own destructive energy. A man will chart the movements of the earth, the appearance of the first cracks, the first fires; observers of the first deaths will be interviewed, so that we may know what to feel. The cameras will move on, there will be studio reconstructions. The whole world will be able to watch its own first convulsions, like a drugged woman in labour, who can see but not feel what is happening to her body. Everybody will sit quietly with their television dinners. Cigarettes and alcohol are coming down in price, just for the duration. There will be pills for sale: pills for narcotic effects, for euphoria, for pain-killing, for death. I as a doctor will be handing them out without prescriptions.

One evening I lie down on the white carpet in our sitting room and a howl comes out of me, like that of a dog, chained, doomed, helpless: 'I don't want to die, I don't want to DIE, I DON'T WANT TO DIE ....' I don't want to die.

The world I have known, green, sunlit, beautiful, is about to become a fiery star. This is happening in my lifetime. I am about to cease to exist.

There is a woman who gives birth to a son in the room in which we are all hiding from death. This is actually one of the university laboratories, built last year, which has abnormally strong walls. I sit at her side, hold her hand, hold her knees apart. At the other end of the great room, people are watching television. A long quiet moan comes from the woman as the child, a small one, slides out on a stream of blood; his head first, his shoulders turning and slippery, his body slim as a fish, grey-blue. I hold him to pump breath into him, to wipe him dry. I have done this many times before, and never before have I thought, this is pointless, pointless, obscene.

Somebody hands pills. News comes from outside, of the many suicides all over the country, all over the world. A woman in Brazil has knifed her six children with a kitchen utensil and then stuck herself in the stomach. In France, twenty people have gassed themselves in a school kitchen. Quietly parents will hand their children the lethal pill; because how can one know, how will one cope, what will it be like, the death that comes suddenly in the night time? It is better to be in control.

And I become possessed with the need for personal salvation. I hold my youngest child upon my knees and we look at books. 'Jackie and Jimmie went down to the sea. There was a man mending boats. Jackie said, I shall be a sailor when I grow up, and Jimmie said, I shall be a fisherman.' This child will never be more than three years old. He says, 'Mummy, can we go to the sea, Mummy, I want to be a fisherman too, Mummy, can I have a fishing net?' And I soothe him as others do, the world over, and murmur lies. Better the lie, better the pill; than that sudden shattering of all faith, all plans and hopes; that fire, terror, destruction, that painful death. And then I notice a man who sits all alone in a straight-backed chair, who is not speaking, not watching television, but simply staring at a fixed spot in space. I wonder at once, what does he see? I hold my child against me and watch the man, waiting for a movement. I fix my mind upon whatever I have heard of God, Christ, resurrection from the dead, I long to believe in it, I strain and strain, as if to reach a state of trance; and nothing changes. I can no longer bear the knowledge that this is all, the end. I can no longer stand the thought, that there is no afterlife. My children? They have not lived. But what is the present? Surely it is the quality, not the quantity, that counts? A seaside holiday, ride upon a donkey in the sun; the knowledge, instinctive, of love and life; might not this be enough? I see the child in the make-shift cradle at its mother's side wave its transparent long-fingered hands like a sea-creature in an aquarium. Is that enough? Or should I have let it die, not rubbed, not blown, not stimulated? I see the curve of the sleeping woman's lips, an absurd animal happiness, as stupidity. We are born, we suffer, we give birth, we die. Angrily I wipe the hot tears from my nose, my chin, and look about for Jem, who has gone to bring us coffee from the machine. More tears pour unwanted, unchecked. It is the hot river dammed by months of self-control; when I did not realise. The little boy says, 'Why are your eyes wet, Mummy?' He does not associate this silent river with unhappiness; for him, crying is screaming and red in the face. I say, nothing, nothing darling, I say it over and over. Outside it is dark now, and the sky appears to be full of fire.

'Excuse me.'

'Oh, thank you. Stupid of me.' I take the handkerchief he offers.

'No, no, not stupid, why aren't we all crying, we should all be in tears, if we realised.'

'Realised what?'

'What you realised just now. That all this beauty, this subtlety, this complexity of evolution, that it is all ending, just like that. That we will end it ourselves, with a little pill.'

'Some people, I suppose, will prefer to wait to the end and take their chance.'

'Will you?'

'I don't know. I don't think I should have the strength. And there are the children, I don't want them to suffer.'

'But aren't you curious? Underneath, don't you want to know what it will be like, the end of the world, the apocalypse, the event for which a thousand generations have waited? Don't you want to see it, the final collapse?'

'I hadn't thought of it from that point of view. Of curiosity.'

'Aren't you curious about death? And what will one understand, if one doses oneself with a pill and simply falls asleep? Nothing.'

I say, 'I don't want to understand death, I just want to live, and if I can't live, then I'll go out the easy way, thank you very much.' And the nangry tears flow and flow, soaking his handkerchief. My little boy sits very still, the picture book fallen from his knee.

The man says, 'Look at me.'

'I'm sorry, yes, look I've soaked your hanky, yes, I know it does no good being hysterical, but you see, I've suppressed it for so long ....'

'Look at me.'

He has a thin face, large grey eyes, an extraordinary serenity and steadiness of gaze. And for all the boniness, his skin seems to have a soft bloom on it, like a very young boy's; at the corners of the eyes, the temples, the corners of the mouth.

'Take my hands.'

His hands hold mine upon his knees with firmness and warmth. I remember now that when they told me at school to pray to God, when I was five — before they took me away, before they realised — I used to think of God as a hand, disembodied, a strong warm male hand holding mine. Once before in my life have I remembered this, my analyst coughed then with discreet appreciation of his own theories. Now, I do not move my hand about nor curl my fingers around his as an adult would, for whom holding hands has an erotic tension all its own, no, I am passive, my hand like a mouse, quiet as a child's.

He says, 'Would you stay alive for me? Keep me company? Not take that pill? Then we would see what we would see together. Together it would not be so bad. Would you trust me?'

I think of Jem, and tension runs into my fingers. 'My husband —'

'Your husband too. You and your husband and your children and I. Trust me. Can you trust me?'

I am still looking at him, still touching him. 'Yes,' I say experimentally. 'Yes, I will trust you.'

And Jem stands there, holding the coffee in plastic cups, burning his fingers. Everything has become all at once very simple. He says to Jem, 'Your wife was the only person in here who was able to cry. I would like to stay with you both, if you don't mind.' And Jem squatting upon his heels on the floor because there is so little room, is at once impressed and silenced by the presence of this man, I see it in his eyes and the tilt of his head. It is now — now — that there seems to be a roaring beginning outside, as if the air whirls thicker and thicker, as if there is storm, tempest, fire, flood, pestilence; it is now that we will feel the building rock, the walls cave, the fire take our bodies; now that the television died in a quick crackle of flame, and men put their hands to their mouths, their wives and children's mouths, now that the suicide pills go down. I am surrounded by the pressing warmth of bodies, Jem's, my children's, the strange man's who held my hand. Outside, it is as if rocks are falling, caught aflame. My mind supplies me with the details, drawn up from the memory that lies within us all. There exists everywhere, in all minds, the archetype for destruction.

I did not expect an epilogue. For the only time in my life, I was conscious of an imminent and sudden end; I believed in it; afterwards one is never the same. There was that moment, and the impossibility of the next one. Nothing afterwards, this I knew.

And next I am walking down a deserted road, I am with Jem and the children and the strange man is no longer with us. I say, deserted; because of the silence after uproar, because of the emptiness after that foetid, crowded room. Buildings stand shattered and empty. I hear an invisible lark sing. There are weeds and scrub growing at the side of the road, but many trees are split and leafless, their branches broken. The road is rough and there are heaps of rubble, boulders. I was once before in a city split by a barren waste of no man's land, where the scrub grew because no foot trod there, I remember the tall marked sides of buildings, the fireplaces and shelves left halfway up. We go on, walking carefully, unable to understand. And then at once I realise: we are left; the world has committed suicide in the night. Out of panic, out of fear, millions have killed themselves. It is the fear that kills, the fear that was all there was to be afraid of. The world has ended, the world we knew; this one, different, scarred, quiet, beginning to breathe again, is another.

And I wake from that roadway to feel the old world build itself around me once again.

SEJOUR EN FRANCE

En vacances

Since it was what she had chosen, she was amazed at its perfection. For usually there was the flaw that seemed to be the result of her choosing; the view just spoiled by a factory chimney, the solitude ruined by a picnicking family, the play or book or film that was not as good as the one that Julia had seen, or Margaret; the truth was, she had begun to think, that she was capable of perceiving quality yet incapable of choosing it. Choosing a holiday, then, had been nearly impossible. Morocco, the man had suggested, Tunisia, Cyprus, Crete. But this foreignness, this utter unfamiliarity was not what she wanted. How did she know what she wanted? How did one do it, spend all one's money on the very thing that one wanted? It was something that she had never done. In the travel agent's office it was already warm and dusty and smelling of foreign money, there was already a tall cactus in a pot, the girl behind the counter was already tanned; only she herself was unready, uncertain of what was going on, feeling her cheque book with her fingers inside her bag and looking about her at all those squares of blue sky. The girl fingered the glass beads, red, blue, green, yellow, red, blue, that went all the way down her throat and into the low white V of her jumper, and her mouth pursed to make a pink cushion. 'You could ask Mr. Golding', she said, 'Or I could give you some brochures, then you could come back when you've made your mind up, couldn't you?'

Mr. Golding, thin-haired in a ginger suit with a waistcoat said 'What about Morocco? Or Tunisia, or Cyprus, or Crete? We have package tours from the first of April. Only you've left it rather late, if you don't mind me saying.'

'I know.' She apologised, too much, and he grew bored; it was familiar. 'But I don't think that's the sort of holiday I really want.'

'Well, madam, until you have decided what sort of holiday you want, I'm afraid I can't help you.'

'Excuse me?'

'You see, madam, it is up to you.' And so she shut her eyes as if seeking an inner vision — just for an instant, there in the patch of winter sunlight on the dusty floor of the travel agent's office, with the smiles and the blue skies and the aeroplanes and sleek ships all around — and at once the conviction appeared. There were the stories, there were the characters; places, visited in a half-dream while the class got on with their work, while she turned a page and paused to look up and repeat, 'Anne, voulez-vous lire, s'il vous plaît?' There was a story of Colette's in which a boy and a girl grow up in love, in a great stern house on the red cliff where thyme grows, and rosemary, and the mountains rise behind, there is a steep sandy way down to the beach, pine trees growing, blue flowers and yellow, a gentle sea drawing back over pebbles, les cailloux, to leave them shining and exposed. She said, just as he was turning his back, 'Wait. I would like to go to the South of France.'

And now she said with the same surprised determination, 'La soupe de poissons, s'il vous plaît. Et puis, je prendrai l'escalope.' Picking up the heavy square of napkin, still slightly damp from the iron. Without the smell of chalk in the air and the langour of adolescent girls around her, it was strange to be speaking French. These were the words from which she made her living. She taught girls to write, read and speak French. And here were people coming and going, men and women, waiters, cooks, even children, all speaking French whether she was there or not. It seemed that her voice had come out loud and forced; she tried again. 'J'aimerai un verre d'eau, s'il vous plaît.' Now, Marianne, Judy, 'Un - verre - d'eau.' Mouths like goldfish, remember; 'd'eau'.' What right had she? But the waiter understood and came back, slopping water on a tin tray.And she spooned up the hot pinkish soup with its sops of bread swimming and thought that only here could she stop being what she was, a teacher of French. The authors she loved would have been at home here, they would have sat like anybody else, drinking soup. She ordered a bottle of wine, forgetting that one could have a half, thinking of Proust, Balzac, particularly Zola. She thought of the descriptions of meals in Zola, and she spooned some more of the hot red rouille into her soup, leaned an elbow on the table in a way she would never have done at home, dipped a crust of bread and sucked its soft end, took a mouthful of the strong pink wine. Here, nobody would have to be forced to read French, nobody would groan or make fun of the language, people would read for pleasure what she told the girls to read for pleasure, the books they had to study for their exams. She looked up, flushed, a middle-aged woman having an early lunch in a rather expensive restaurant near the port in a little French fishing town and resort. The waiter hardly noticed her, thought only, the tourists are coming early this year and I had better get those tables outside cleared because it is going to rain. Outside, the plane trees began to move their short pruned branches in the wind, but still the rattle of the shrouds and the bump-bump of the boats' bows could not be heard inside the safe, heated restaurant. She began to wish she had been more adventurous, had the speciality rather than the veal, which one could after all eat inland. At home, she would not have eaten veal, on account of the way calves were reared; here, a vague impression that the French did things differently and better upheld her until the dish arrived; and then the smell, the crisp brownness, the sizzle under the drops from a fat wedge of lemon did the rest. She did not look up from her plate to see how the sky had darkened over the bay, how the tall red cliff had vanished into cloud, how the boats in the harbour lashed at each other with their tied masts, and the men pulled the nets in quickly, and the rest-auranteurs whipped check tablecloths from tin tables and stacked striped umbrellas and ran about, washing up cloths tucked at their waists, shooing children indoors, shouting and pulling faces at the fishermen. When she had arrived, that very morning, she had seen how the sky was a clear, pale blue with only ribbed patches of cloud, patterned like fish skeletons, hanging near the sun; how the light was all dappled, how like — she thought gleefully — to an im-pressionist painting, with the light and dark of the mottled, partly peeling planes, their pale tucked leaves just emerging against whiter twigs, and the light cast upon the bottoms of the rocking boats, mottling them too as the ripples moved upon the water, and the dark squares of netting, the shining bodies of the fish; it had all been a whole, a perfect whole, a square picture between the houses, filled with stippled light;

that she had been there to observe and claim it had been the most miraculous. She ate, and took great mouthfuls of the wine, with the picture from an hour ago to be held in her mind forever. Even the noise — shouts, greetings, children's screams, hooting cars, the high whine of the little motorbikes — had not been there to spoil but to intensify it, bringing it vividly alive. At home, at school, anywhere else, she hated noise. She and Julia Gimson, standing in the staff room at coffee time, leaning as if their legs would no longer carry them; 'Honest to God, I don't think I can stand another minute. The little wretches in 4B were so noisy, I couldn't get them to settle. I think I've got another headache coming on.' 'Never mind, dear, only a week and it's the end of term.' And there was the boy downstairs who had just got himself a bike, a big one; its noise splitting open her planned peace as she sat with her coffee, reading in the evening. There, she did not think of noise as signifying life, only intrusion; or perhaps it was only sometimes that one actually wanted life to intrude. And as she sat over her lunch, thinking at that very moment how pleasant it was not to be intruded upon, the door of the restaurant flew open, letting in what seemed to be a packet of wet black mackintosh. The wind curled instantly around her, picked up the corners of the table cloth, made her shiver. When the door slammed shut, her heavy fork clattered to the floor, and she did not think that she had dropped it.

'Pardon, Madame. Je m'excuse.' She had bent to retrieve it, she had to, for there was still one mouthful of the veal upon her plate; but he met her halfway and handed it back, and several drops fell from his wet head upon her sleeve.

'Merci, monsieur.'

'Je vous en prie.' How correct the French were, how they knew how to behave. 'You must not forget that French has always been the language of diplomacy. Are you listening, Jane? Diplomacy. It has a subtlety that is not to be found in English. English may be verbally richer, but French has more finesse.'

'C'est à vous, aussi?' It was her scarf, the silk one patterned with birds, that had slipped to the floor.

'Merci, monsieur.' 'Dict'e; Tout soudain, je me suis rendue compte que mon foulard ... Foulard, Jenny, no I will not repeat it, you will have to listen more carefully.'

'Quel sale de temps, non?' She was almost sure that this was an expression that one did not use; she treasured it doubtfully in her mind. 'Please, Miss Hastings, what does 'dégeulasse' mean?' Marianne had been to Paris for a holiday, Marianne had a French stepfather. 'I think it is a word that you need not use in your essay, Marianne.' But she need not have feared, he had seated himself quite ordinarily at a far table, in the corner, nearest to the kitchen. He did not bother to read the menu, but sat relaxed, his forearms on the table, his big fingers playing with the glass. Without asking, the waiter set before him a carafe of rosé with a chipped edge, and a basket of bread. His soup arrived next, without having been asked for. Miss Hastings waited for the waiter to return to her, her face turned in his direction; unconsciously she moved her pointed, eager face to follow his movements, as a dog watches those of the person who feeds him. And the man in the corner sucked up his soup and watched Miss Hastings, without much interest, because she was the only other person in the room. She thought, when I have had my dessert and my coffee, I will go at once. Lunch, which had been leisurely, a delicious waste of time, became all

179

at once a meal to be over with. She must use her time sensibly. A walk along the beach, a look at the town's monuments, the church; she must not, after all, spend her time in solitary greed.

'C'était bon, madame?'

'C'était tres bien, monsieur.'

'Alors, on a des fruits, du fromage, des glaces, du flan caramel — ?'

'Du fromage, s'il vous plaît.' It seemed less self-indulgent, more plainly functional a choice. She would have been ashamed now to have ordered an ice. And the cheese when it came was an exact rectangle of gruyère, as if it were the last piece in the house.

The man in the corner wiped his mouth with his checked napkin and broke off a piece of bread. He said, 'You ought to try the local cheeses, the little Provençal ones, very soft they are, made with herbs.' He spoke with the strong, rolling accent of the Midi.

'Excuse me? Oh, but I like gruyère.' She cut off too large a slice and put it in her mouth, making it impossible for herself to speak; regretted it, only too late.

'Oh, but one should also try what one does not know already. Do you not think so?'

A big mouthful of water; but there was only wine; she could not speak, but swallowed the cooled wine in a great gulp. He watched.

'Are you on holiday, madame?'

'Yes.' Recovered, only slightly pink, she faced him. He was about thirty-five, not more, a heavy dark-haired man, his face brown with wind and sun, he did not sit up straight to eat, but lounged, looking at her between mouthfuls, talking when his mouth was full of bread. The waiter brought a dish of seafood with rice and the smell reached Miss Hastings' nostrils and made the juices pour into her mouth, although she had only just eaten. It must be the gruyère, a sharp cheese, too stimulating to the palate. She watched, wishing that she had chosen the seafood after all. Tomorrow. This is a real Frenchman, she thought suddenly, this is the object I have tried so often to describe. La France is the centre of European civilisation. En France on mange bien. Monsieur Dupont va au bureau, Madame Dupont fait ses courses; traduisez, Jenny, s'il vous plaît. They had never been to France, except for Marianne who watched with slight scorn from the back of the class. For them, France was something she had invented for them to learn about. On holiday, they went to Majorca, to Greece, even to North Africa. They flew to places, on package tours with their parents. Their parents saw no point in stopping so near home, in France. And so they absorbed, piecemeal, her archaic vision of France. They learned of a country whose government was laughably volatile when compared to the British, yet which specialised in diplomacy, a certain savoir faire; a country which had twice been saved by the British and was therefore grateful and admiring; a place which had long been the cradle of European civilisation and rational thought, which was even now a distillation of Versailles, Descartes, the gallant failing monarchy, the Belle Epoque. In France, people came home from work on bicycles, carrying baguettes; there was no processed food; sexual morality, though not mentioned overtly, was interestingly flexible. From Miss Hastings, they absorbed the atmosphere of Proust's corklined room, the social hierarchies of Combray; with her they shared the search for La Domaine Perdu through the dense green hardly-lit forests of central France; they knew of Toulouse-Lautrec, Modigliani, l'Inconnue de la Seine: for something of her own longing reached them, that was why they listened, only pretending to yawn; underneath the grammar and the dictée and the reading round the class on hot summer afternoons they heard a real note of deprivation, they knew there was something which they, young and with all their opportunities, must not miss. To each other they said, dismissing it, 'She does go *on*', and replied, half listening, 'You can tell she's an old maid.' They could not guess that though they married and had children and pursued fulfilling careers, something of Miss Hastings' longing would remain with them, making them wake up one day unsettled, wondering what they lacked. Where was this country that she had described, that she had made them learn about so assiduously? It had little to do with autoroutes and supermarches, with Gaullisme or a police force armed with gas. It was the lost, perfect distillation of the French past that she offered them. She told them of a place which they, as adults, would never be able to find.

But she was unaware, she never considered, she knew that by some people's standards her teaching methods were old-fashioned, but they passed exams, the French aurals results last year were good, their accents were not too bad;

she knew that they were essential to her,
otherwise she would not be able to go on
teaching French. Now, she could hardly
remember why she had begun to teach French.
An aptitude at school, a facility for languages;
university, a month or two spent in Paris. But
had there been a summer beach, a forgotten
stretch of coast, where a cliff ran down red into
the sea, where thyme grew, and rosemary; a
house, cool, many-roomed with red tiled floors,
where adolescents drank watered wine and
scuffed their feet in sandshoes and held hands
while the adults played patience and looked
away? Had this been her youth, or another's?
She could not remember. The pink wine and all
the food had made her sleepy, made her forget.
He had asked her something, she must reply.

'Yes,' she said, 'I'm a French teacher.' Surely
the rain must stop now; there were these freak
storms she knew, on the south coast, but they
could not last as long as this. She wanted to
leave; she had finished her coffee, the bill was
before her, folded, placed between the salt and
pepper pots. She had brought no mackintosh
and even her coat was at the hotel. In this rain
she would be soaked in a moment. Outside, a
table clattered to the tarmac, its legs folding

under it, and the rain sluiced horizontally across the pavement. The sky was a wild dark grey, sliced with greenish light over the sea. In England one might say, 'Ah, I think it must be going to clear'; but here there was no knowing. All the signs were unfamiliar, unknown, all the ways in which one might predict the weather had been taken away.

The man in the corner, seeing her discomfort, said, 'One might as well pass the time pleasantly. May I join you, Madame? May I offer you something as a digestif? A cognac, perhaps? It seems that we shall be prisoners here for a while.'

She looked at him, scared. The waiter said, 'I'm sorry, Madame, it is another ten francs.'

'Oh, I'm sorry, I thought it was twenty. Thirty francs, is it really thirty francs?' Agitation mounted in her throat; she had been extravagant; she did not even want to be here, in this restaurant; it had all been a mistake. She should have been sensible and bought a sandwich and eaten it in her room. The waiter stood very near, until the black-haired man with an impatient, even angry gesture, shooed him away. 'Two cognacs, François. And forget the rest.'

'Shall I put it on your bill, then?'

'Yes, yes, you charge too much anyway, it's a disgrace.' Miss Hastings began to protest, claustrophobia threatened, she could not bear that he should have the right to sit here, having paid part of her bill. And then she said to herself, he is a Frenchman, a real Frenchman; and she tried to relax. The cognac came in tiny gold-rimmed glasses, very light to hold, and it burned the end of her tongue. It would not be too difficult. They could talk of French civilisation, books, the theatre; and then the rain would stop. The waiter stood at the door scowling, for nobody else would come to eat in this weather. He took off his apron, wiped his hands on it and threw it across the bar. The black-haired man dismissed Racine with a wave of his hand, as he had dismissed the waiter. His hair grew very low on his neck, and his neck was sunburned all the way down into his navy blue jersey. His hands spanned the table, moving salt and pepper pots, rearranging everything as he spoke. He said that he was, had been, an engineer, but that now he preferred to hire out boats to tourists and to take them in his motor launch up the coast. And the time moved on, the sky began to clear, the drops that fell to spurt from the cobbles were only those from the soaked awning. The waiter went outside with a long stick and prodded the centre of the awning, where it ballooned with water, so that suddenly sheets of rain hit the pavement, like the burst of the last cloud. She began to tell the story in her mind already; of the fascinating Frenchman with whom she had whiled away the afternoon drinking cognac while the mediterranean storm raged outside. Beyond the glass door, a miraculous light was spreading. It was as if a layer had been peeled from reality. She gazed, and he saw her, it stopped him in mid-sentence. 'Yes,' he had been saying, 'I think it will fine this afternoon, quand même.'

When she turned to face him he was surprised by her face; still middle-aged, sandy, pale-eyed; yet radiant. He could not think what she had seen, that could have changed her. Yes, she was thinking, and we talked for most of the afternoon, the rain was bucketing down outside, he told me all about himself, this Frenchman, Maurice his name was — for she would have discovered, they would have confessed — and, one really only gets to know a country through getting to know its inhabitants; and then suddenly the sky cleared. It was the colour of a blackbird's egg, there was a miraculous light over everything. She felt herself, she knew herself now; as a mature woman to whom things like this might happen. She should have come to France before.

'I suppose,' she said easily, 'It must be quite ordinary for you. I mean, you must have got used to it, this sudden change in weather, having lived here all your life. But for an English person, it is extraordinary.'

'Oh, I haven't lived here all my life,' he said, in his perfect French, tinged with the accent of Marseille, she thought, 'I was born in Sydney, Australia. I'm Australian. I've only been here a year or two. Did you think I was French?'

'But your accent, your French —' her voice had become a whisper, it was all she could say. 'I mean, your French is very good.' Ten out of ten, top of the class; she heard herself with distaste.

All he would say was, 'Well, it's easy enough to pick up.' And the rain had stopped; there was the sun. There was no point in saying anything else. She picked up her bill and her scarf and left the restaurant with him, and outside they smiled at each other and each lifted a hand, and they went off in opposite directions. Australian.

Only outside the little church did she stop, breathe, hear the violent thudding of her own heart. She was in a narrow little street that had come steeply uphill from the harbour and the earthen walls rose on both sides of her, there were the iron gates to overgrown gardens drenched with rain, and the numbers of houses written white upon blue in iron; there was steam in the air and a chirping and humming all around; warmth was held between the walls, water shone still upon the stones; and there was this smell, that held her still and attentive. The church stood yellow in the new sunlight, its closed doors waiting to be pushed open to admit her into darkness. She would not go in, not yet. She stood, waiting to catch the scent again, and moved a few steps forward, was flooded by it; understood that she could only catch it by moving, that one only knew that one had smelled it once it was past. It was something in there, something hidden behind those walls, in one of those locked gardens; not pine. not herbs, not lilac or mimosa; something more wonderful than either. She walked up and down and could not find the scent again anywhere in the roadway; only when she decided to leave it and walk on was she once again held, trapped by it.

This time, she walked on up the hill and towards the church, firmly. Once one had experienced something, it was one's own, whatever happened next. It would have been a mistake to have gone back.

Years later, when she was quite old, she came across that particular smell again and discovered that it was the rare combination of a charcoal fire with wet wisteria in full bloom. But at the time, it did not matter; it could remain unnamed; she walked on up the hill with the springy tread of a young woman, to reach the little church. It was still only the first day of her holiday.

En voyage

It was still hot; but after the heat of the train, the closeness to people, this sea air that just lifted locks of hair and dried patches of sweat was in itself a relief. He wanted a drink. The plastic Evian water bottle, filled a day ago with tepid water from a bathroom tap, was nearly empty. It would be like drinking from a radiator. His mother had it tucked away somewhere, among the crumbs of old picnics and the stale, carefully filled waves of picnics yet to come. She was talking, busy; she would not want him to ask for a drink now. And so he moved his tongue about in his mouth and it felt large and rough, dry as pumice stone. He thought of dry bread, the yolks of hard-boiled eggs, pastry: in order to

191

discover if he felt sick. The crowd was moving forward, inches at a time, towards the sea; there was one narrow passageway between the station and the quay, one gangway for climbing up to the boat. But above the heads, through the gaps as people moved along, there was that air, that breeze carrying salt. Soon he would stand at the white rail and look down into the churned depths of the green sea; feel spray upon his cheek; close his eyes to feel the movement that was nearly sickness, that was weakness only just held at bay.

His mother said, 'Are you feeling all right, Oliver?' Sharpish, pushing him along with the corner of her suitcase. His nose was at the level of the armpits of others. She said, 'Don't wander along with your eyes shut, you'll get lost. Come on, we're moving.' A few yards forward, the shuffle and the shifting of the bags. Everybody kept their eyes fixed straight ahead, ignored each other. Except for his mother, who chattered to the man at her side, 'You'd think they could organise it a bit better than this, wouldn't you? It's incredible. It's taken us half an hour to get off that train.' Except for the man, who looked down at her, probably liked her tousled hair, her vivid eyes ringed with black, murmured something in sympathy, was about to ask her where she had stayed. It had been like that in the railway carriage, they had all sat staring straight ahead, suffering the heat of the compartment, the wait at Paris, the clatter of the trolleys in the corridor; until his mother had moved; dropped something, he could not remember, exclaimed, offered cigarettes, opened the window. And then they had all started to chatter, as she did. He sat with his legs stuck stiffly before him, his trousers too tight. You never see a French boy in baggy trousers, she had said; he pulled his jersey down in case the zip might split. And there was a girl sitting opposite him, a French girl reading a magazine. She ate her way through a pile of grapes, pips and all, and occasionally she put down the magazine and laughed aloud; but nobody asked her why. Yes, a woman said, it was the same thing in Spain. We've just come from Madrid. Marvellous trains, but never running on time. Another said, folding her arms — low bosom flattened in pink knitted silky stuff, freckles on the arms, a flabbiness above the elbow tightened as she clasped her breast — impossible, oh, I could never sleep in a train; not a wink; never; out of the question; I would rather sit up all night. Oliver's mother, animated, pleased with herself, ran the conversation; she began to tell in her lightest tone the story of herself and Oliver's father in a casino in the south. Near Saint-Raphael, we were staying. The cicadas, the air, the wonderful south. And then a man came up to us and told us .... And my husband, my late husband — I am recently widowed, you see — said .... But of course, things change so quickly. Oliver would never know — and she ran a hand through his hair, caressing him as if it were something she often did. You must be so proud of him, a handsome boy. And he's going to his father's old school. Yes, in the autumn. Oh, he's looking forward to it, aren't you, darling? The train had been hell.

'Ollie, are you sure you're all right? Have one of those seasick pills, darling, better to be safe than sorry.'

'No thank you. I'm fine.'

'Oh, look, they're beginning to move along, at last. Honestly, these French officials, they're stuck in their own red tape.' She repeated the phrase to the man on her left, added, 'God knows what it'll be like when we join the Common Market. I mean, I adore France, but —

Oliver thought, it is wrong to dislike one's mother; yet surely it is worse to pretend? Is it possible to love somebody and at once find her boring, embarrassing, vulgar, tactless? Do I have to love her? Is there no other choice? He looked at her now. He tried to pretend that he saw her for the first time, that he was another boy, a foreign boy, not hers. He examined her from close to — as they paused upon the gangplank, as the few feet of sea swished beneath them — her wild black hair that blew in the wind, her tan, accentuating the wrinkles, as she had read while lying in the sun, her make-up, red lips, black pencil, a smudge of eyeshadow that made her eyes smoky, the blue that rises first from a new fire. She stood at the rail, the ship achieved, she held him at her side and made him look back towards France, finding romance even in the cranes and grey buildings of Calais Maritime. She said, whispering in his ear, forcing him again to share her sentiment, 'Goodbye, France.' Her breasts swelled out above the confines of her bra, under the white sweater; her French jeans clung to every curve of her bottom and thighs; her hand, brown, ringed, nails polished, lay upon the warm railing, upon white peeling paint. The trouble was, she was still young. Thirty-six to his twelve years. He was helpless before her, he saw even strong men become helpless. The one with the wall eye, now, who had carried her case up the gangplank and set it down with a smile — oh, he knew that smile — at her feet.

'Look', she said, 'Look, Ollie, we're sailing.' And once he would have shared her excitement, at the ship's movement, the sudden sheet of water between ship and land, at the whole scene upon the quay and the people clustering at the rail; he would have been caught up without a murmur into her zest for it all, for life. Now he thought, she is a fake, she cannot really be feeling that. It's only an old channel ferry, why must she behave as if she's sailing to America, for God's sake. His nails picked at the flaking paint, he would not look towards the shore. She assumed too much; that he had no feeling, no interpretation of his own. And yet she was right, he had none. He waited for her to act, to move; she had not allowed him, ever, to respond first. But how vague these thoughts were, how inchoate. He felt it all, but as a pain trapped somewhere below his collarbone, shut within the confines of his chest. There was nothing, no reason, no explanation; she was attractive, intelligent, people liked her, she was unlike other mothers, one could see that at a glance; why must she cause him this constant pain? A phrase came into his head, but he dared not say it. It rang and rang, like a persistent caller at a front door bell. It said, 'Why can't you grow up? Why can't you grow up?' And he suppressed it, refused to answer, never cried out that he wanted to be allowed to be a child, now, for the last time, before the autumn and his father's school. She put a hand over his now, she held his damp fingers tight. He could feel all the vibration of her body, coming down into that hand; he made his hand small and helpless, to escape, he swallowed hard but the pain remained in his chest, choking him. She said, 'God, I could never get tired of this. Travel. Leaving places, arriving in new places. Boats, going in and out of harbours. How lucky you are, to have so much of life before you.' He thought, I shall be a bank clerk, an insurance man, to punish you. But aloud he said, 'Could I have one of those pills, after all? I do feel a bit weird. And have we still got any of that water?' If she was disappointed in him she rarely showed it, he would give her that; but her enthusiasm for other things, other people, carried her along, she had no time to express disappointment in a person who hardly mattered to her. He wondered sometimes how his father, that quiet man, had felt.

'Why did you say you were a widow?' It came out, sheer as a hiccup, he had not planned it. 'Why did you say that about Dad, and make them think he was dead?'

'Oh, for God's sake, Ollie, why d'you have to be so literal? Dead, divorced, what difference does it make? One's only talking to people on a train.'

He thought, to me it matters; but no picture of his father, to cheer him, appeared; there was only an Identikit face, eyes, nose, mouth, ears, a thatch of light brown hair; it had all been too long ago. He said, 'Is it okay to tell lies on trains, then?' He made himself sound younger than he was, he said, 'Is it okay, then, when you're travelling?' But she did not answer. She lit a Gauloise, puffed acrid smoke over him, glanced at him with her blue eyes narrowed. He understood her anger perfectly; it was what he wanted, he knew now. Nothing happened un-intentionally, after all. What he had wanted was to stop her gazing towards that strip of vanishing land like somebody in a film, to stop her pretending. His voice, to achieve it, had become babyish on its own. And he knew, seeing her narrowed eyes upon him, that she was capable of hatred for him too. She said, 'Why don't you go and look round the ship. Most boys of your age would be dying to look at the engine room.' Making it into a criticism. He said, listless now that he had achieved his aim, ruffled her, 'Okay'.

'And don't get lost. I'll wait for you here. I'm going to have a drink.' And she got out her half-finished bottle of wine, her packet of sand-wiches, squatting down like a gypsy, uncurling on to the deck like somebody who really wanted to be alone with a picnic and a good book. He saw men's eyes upon her. He thought, why can they not see that she is ridiculous? Tired of it all, he wandered off among the passengers, into the rocking interior of the boat.

'Hi.' The voice at his ankles made him jump. 'You nearly trod on me', it said, uncritically.

'I'm sorry. I'm terribly sorry, I didn't see you. Sorry, I thought there was nobody here.' In the hold, a secret place, dark and stacked with coils of rope. He saw the man's white teeth shine; he would never forget the extraordinary whiteness of those perfectly even teeth. 'Looking for a place for a quiet smoke?' The voice, American surely, with a laughing sound behind it.

'No. No, I don't. Actually, I was just looking round. The boat, you know. Actually, I was just trying to get away from my mother.' Yet nothing that just popped out like that was an accident; his new discovery filled him with alarm. It was as if he had suddenly lost control over what he said.

'Oho,' said the American, 'Parent trouble. Well, I can tell you, if I had my mother along, I'd be trying sure as hell to get away from her. D'you like nuts? Here, I got these in Barcelona.'

'Barcelona? I've never been to Spain. We just rented a house in the south of France.'

'Wow. You must be a duke or something, are you?'

'No. No.' It would not do to say, my mother's friend, the Frenchman who owned it, I don't think we paid actually, I think it was just borrowed. He said, 'We're going back to London now. I have to go back to school. I've only got the summer term, and then I'm going to boarding school.'

'Christ', said the American, 'I'm glad I've got that education bit over with. You get out of school and you're free, you know that?'

'Oh, no', Oliver said, 'I mean, you have to get a job, and things. Have a career. Surely that's worse. Unless you're a woman', he added, 'I suppose you can do what you like then.' Borrow houses, take money from a man you no longer love, tell strangers lies upon trains.

'Well, I do what I like, and I'm not a woman.'

'No, oh no. Do you really?' In the gloom, away from the sunlight, his eyes gradually became accustomed. He saw a beard, curly hair springing wildly all over pointed ears, a broad brown forehead, large grey eyes with clear whites and long lashes, a wide mouth smiling to show those astonishing teeth; wrinkles of amusement, lines of acceptance. 'What do you do?' he said. Whatever it was, it would be the only thing worth doing.

'Well, nothing, right now. I'm just travelling.'

'But what for?'

'Just to see the world. What else?'

'That's all my mother wants to do,' he said, disappointed.

'Well, what's wrong with that? In my experience, mothers generally just want to stay home and make you buckle down to something, make you swallow some shit about earning an honest penny.'

'But don't you have to?'

'Well, I'll come clean. I'm a university teacher, back in the states. I'm taking a year off, it's called a sabbatical.'

'You can't be a teacher. You're too —' he wanted to say, 'young'; instead he said, 'beautiful'. He had never said anything so embarrassing in his life; he blushed, bit his lip, turned his face to hide in the shadow of the rope pile. But the man only laughed, said, 'Wowee, that's nice', and fished about in his rucksack to produce a bottle of olives.

'D'you like olives?'

He did not, but said, 'Yes.'

'I got these in Marseille. They're really good. Have one. I think I've even got a bit of wine left, we could wash them down with that.'

'How will I get them out?' They were at the bottom of the jar, in dirty liquid, lying fat and black and wrinkled, like slugs.

'Here.' The American pulled out a knife from his bag; at first it was no more than a slim penknife that he saw, blades invisible; and then there was a click and a gleaming thin spike shot out, that reached almost to his chest; he drew back, winced, the American said, 'Never seen a flick knife before? I got this in Naples. Come on, take it, you can spike the olives one at a time.'

'I think they're illegal in England.' He took the handle delicately, inserted the blade to find an olive as he was told.

'Flick knives? Never mind, I'll only be in England a few days. I won't pull it on any old ladies, I promise you. Have some wine? This is Spanish, it's pretty rough, I warn you.'

The sour, dark taste of the olive; the wash of warm wine afterwards; how would he ever accept either again? There was a rankness, an aftertaste that could never be forgotten. At school he would say, 'I often had black olives washed down with red wine. Spanish stuff. Pretty rough, I can tell you.' He handed back the knife. He gazed at the American in alcoholic ecstasy. The longing to be a child, to behave as a child, was quite gone, forever. Now, there was only the need to be a man. He said, 'Tell me about where you've been. You know, travelling to see the world. What sort of things did you see?'

'Well, I guess all kinds of things. Shall I tell you about a fight I saw in Marseille last night?'

'We were in Marseille last night. We never saw a fight.'

'No, well, you have to be in the right place at the right time. That's what it's all about.'

'Tell me. What happened? Was anyone killed?'

'Well, it was like this. I was in this cafe, I was just having a brandy, late last night —' He saw the darkened cafe, the street lights, the man alone, the drunken sailors who came in; and the fat man behind the bar, drying glasses, his lips pursed. He heard the laughter, felt the tension rise in the air, saw the knife suddenly slip out, change hands; heard the crash of falling furniture, saw the slow silent seep of blood afterward upon the sleeve of a shirt, the drops that fell to the floor. Heard the wail of police car sirens, the laconic tones of the Marseille police, the screams from a woman who stood at a doorway, who wound and wound her hands in her apron, unable to believe it at all. That was what it was all about.

'But why did the man at the bar give the knife to the drunk?'

'Search me. It was the craziest thing I've ever seen. But it was a hell of a piece of luck that the guy only got it in the arm, if he'd have gotten it in the gut there'd have been real trouble. Hey, are you all right? You look a bit green to me.'

'Yes. I guess so.' Unconsciously his speech fell into the pattern of the American's. 'I guess it might have been the wine, though.'

'Come on, let's go on deck and get a breath of air. This boat is beginning to roll a bit.'

They stood side by side at the rail on the lower deck; Oliver remembered his mother with her picnic and her paperback on the upper, camping like a student among her possessions. 'I ought to get back to my mother before we arrive.' France was gone now, England a thickening line amid cloud. But he did not want to sound concerned; he said, 'Still, I guess there's half an hour or so before we're in Dover.'

'Guess so.' The American did not sound interested in their arrival. He leaned on the railing, his brown arms bare to the elbow supporting his chin. Oliver did the same. Beneath them the sea turned back its white edge at the ship's side; the spray rose and slapped them in the face, the wind came at them in snatches and Oliver saw the American's thick hair as a bush that grew on a windswept hilltop, dense as gorse or furze; his own, thin, brown, straight and rather long, blew flat against his cheeks.

The American said, 'Isn't it great?' and Oliver agreed thoughtlessly until he remembered his mother, her pointless enthusiasms. He said, 'Well, it must be really something if you're going on a long sea voyage. That'd be exciting.'

The American looked at him strangely. 'I don't mean where we're going, or where we've come from,' he said. 'I mean, just this. The colour of the sea, the wind, the feeling of being on deck. Still, if you don't get it, you don't.'

'Oh, I do.' But what he meant was that to be here with him, that strong careless easy-going man at his side, that was great. Feeling his own weakness, his incapacity, he said, 'You get out of practise at just enjoying things. It's being at school, I suppose.'

There was silence, as if he was neither heard nor understood. Then, after minutes, the man beside him turned his head as if he had only just heard, looked at him searchingly — grey eyes with black centres, a faint ring of green — and said, 'Oh, sure. Everybody has a damn good go at getting you out of practice. But you ain't got to let them. D'you know, once I was in a Jesuit school. I don't suppose that means much to you. I was reared in a rich family in the southern states of America. I was all set to be a southern gentleman — before I lit out, that was. You can be damn sure all those jokers had a go at getting me out of practice. But after I quit the whole establishment, I began to realise what the whole good of life was. It was while I was in Europe just for a short time. I was a college kid, still conventional as hell. The first time I was in Paris. That's where all good Americans go first. I met a man in a bar. I can't even remember what he said to me. But the sense of it stuck. It sounds trivial, just enjoy things, but I don't mean it that way. No sweat, that's all. You may die tomorrow.'

You may die tomorrow. It had simply never occurred to Oliver before. But at twelve years old, with no experience of freedom; no knife fights in bars, no squatting on a rope coil eating nuts brought from Barcelona, to be somewhere for a couple of days and then on to somewhere else; no travelling this world just to see it, with a rucksack, a flick knife, a half-empty bottle of wine. He stared, and the wind blew up gusts of spray to dash the tears from his eyes. He fixed his eyes upon the brown hand that lay so easily next to his upon the rail, and could not bear that it should ever be withdrawn.

The American said, 'Hey, it looks as if we're nearly in.' And real cliffs, bright green grass, ranks of tidy little red houses had already appeared.

'So soon?' Oliver looked up, hating England, wanting for the first time in his life the security of endless travel.

'What about your mother?'

'Oh, hell, yes. But I must go back and get my book. I left it down by the rope coils. Could you wait here a moment?'

The American nodded, showing faint surprise at being expected to wait. And the crowds pushed against Oliver as he dived through to the hold, he was held up by legs and bodies and suitcases; he was away far longer than he had thought to be, and the book, when he found it, was already not worth the trouble; a book such as a boy would read who had nothing better to look at. Clutching it, he scrambled back, up the brown polished stairs and the inscription that said the 'Marie-Helene' had been launched first in 1948, his hand leaping up the ornate banister, past the lounges and the restaurant and smell of French cooking that hung in the air, past the closed duty free shops, past the bar where a man already swept up cigarette ends, stacked glasses, washed up for the return journey. The boat was already in dock, but the crowds milled helplessly to and fro, barging towards the single gangplank that would let them off. Oliver looked at the place where he had left his friend, saw a man in a long tan overcoat, a woman in a pink headscarf, suitcases piled one upon another. They returned coolly his panicking stare. He was gone. He was gone forever. There was only England, school, mother, ordinary life. The pain returned to his chest, he would choke with it, he struggled and could not breathe, And then, 'There you are!' He heard the shout, 'Hey, Oliver!' How had he known his name? He looked up, past the shoulders of other people and their heads against the sky. Two faces looked down on him from the upper deck, two tanned, smiling faces with curling hair that rose in dark crests against the wind. His mother and the American. 'Hey, I found your mother!' his friend shouted, 'Come up and join us, we thought you'd been crushed to death. It'll be hours before this lot get off.'

'Ollie!' his mother waved a hand that held a Gauloise, smiled her encouragement to him, 'Come on, you look as if you'd seen a ghost!' And the American showed his white teeth in that smile — that smile that Oliver knew so well. Tears springing from his eyes, soaking his cheeks, he turned and fumbled back into the ship's interior, returning in the way he had come.

A la montagne

'But why do we have to go to the top?' James felt that where he was, sitting upon soft pine needles, his back against a pine that poured resinous smells into his nostrils, each boot upon a large flat stone, was good enough.

'Well —'

'Don't say, because it's there.'

'Well, I just feel like going to the top. One just does, with mountains.'

'I don't.' Tennis-playing: incompetent. Chess: haphazard. Gardening: lazy. Driving: speedy but not aggressive. He searched in his mind through her usual activities for a clue to this sudden desire to conquer a mountain, and found none. No great physical energy, but bouts of enthusiasm; and then the sudden flinging down of the racquet — 'Oh, I've had enough!' and the sudden desire for a coffee just when he had manoeuvred his queen. No apparent ambition, nothing steady; the only thing she had really stuck at was the oboe, and languages were anyway a natural gift. He looked at her through lowered lashes — so lazy, he felt, so content and lazy, just to be here — and thought how sunburn suited her, and the slight rim of sweat upon her lip, and the lack of pencil around her brilliant blue eyes. Her hair flopped upon her forehead and she pushed it back. It flopped again, and she pushed it again. He said tenderly, 'You're hot, have a rest. Go on, lie down here, it's lovely.'

'Well, just for a minute. But I think it'll take us most of the afternoon, to get to the top and down again before the bus goes.'

'Oh, damn the top. Here, have some water. And there's some chocolate in my pocket, we might as well eat it before it melts.' Perhaps it was that no real challenge had been offered to her, in her life with him; perhaps it was simply that before, no mountain had appeared. He thought about it, the process of thought these days like the very slow rewinding of a tape recorder, one thing after another moving simply through his mind. No challenge, so no ambition. Or did ambition precede challenge? The thought stopped, jammed. He closed his eyes completely and moved the back of his head into the slight indentation in the tree's trunk that might have been made for him. Beyond the immediate red of his own inner eye, there was the pattern of dark furred pine branches against a dark blue sky. Beyond that sky, there was more sky. He was small, helpless, he did not care; he could not move. The wine they had drunk for lunch made his fingers heavy and his toes huge inside his boots. The chocolate made a dry crust upon his palate and joined his lips together; but there was always the plastic bottle of Evian water to moisten them again.

'Well —?'

'Well what?'

'Shall we go on?'

'Do we have to?'

'Think of the view from the top.'

'But look at the view from here.' White rounded stones where they sat, pines, herb bushes, flame bushes, lilac; a short fall of stone and then a fertile valley, changing by the minute with spring sunshine.

'I know, but let's go on.' He said nothing, but listened for a moment to the far distance; somewhere between the dim sound of traffic upon the only road and the close sharpness of her voice, there was a regular tap-tap upon wood. A woodpecker, drilling. An unseen bird in the depths of a cool forest. A woodpecker doing the only thing that woodpeckers had to do. He thought, she will accuse me, in her head if not aloud. There is so much we do not know about each other. Curiosity, energy are supposed to be the male characteristics; she is still waiting for me to show them. And what of her? I never knew, for one thing, that she would climb mountains. They had only been married for a year.

'Charlotte?'

'Yes?'

'I'll come to the top with you if you like.' But she took it quite calmly as if it had already been decided. She stood up at once and threw back her black hair and gave him her hand. Pretending to be old and stiff, he made her pull him up. And they leaned together against the pine tree, in each other's arms, laughing. James thought, perhaps at the top of the mountain we will make love. The path was narrow, and to begin with he led the way and she followed, one step in front of another, one step in front of another, carefully, slowly, without speaking much; through small copses of trees that grew straight out of rock, rose bushes, wild holly, great knotted trees of rosemary flowering blue, gorse bushes, little oak trees, the old whitened pines. They walked for a while as if he were the leader and she followed, and because their minds were absent, dawdling elsewhere, and only their feet moved regularly on, this seemed for the time being to be entirely natural.

'James.' He heard the exasperation in her voice and turned. 'Don't go striding on like an automaton.'

'I thought you wanted to get to the top.'

'Yes, but we don't have to *plod* so. Look, I found this, I wanted to show you, and you were just *plodding* ahead.

He laughed, in spite of himself, at this picture of himself. 'Plodding? Do you expect me to fly?' He pirouetted in his thick boots, waved a leg in the air, flapped his arms, 'Beat you to the top, in that case.' He felt light, he was ridiculous; he was happy. In the dirty palm of her sunburned hand she showed him a perfect white shell. 'D'you think the sea can ever have possibly come in this far?' Baffled, they both turned as if to question it, that glittering strip that lay against the sky down there. The wind from the sea cooled their faces as they turned, and they felt how the sun had burned them. Suddenly they were high up, suddenly alone. The peaks of Haute Provence waited, they all seemed to face in the same direction and were beaked, like birds. It was a serious moment. But she broke it in a second, she ran and scrambled ahead of him, tripping sometimes over small plants, righting herself like a horse that stumbles, with a jerk of her thick mane. 'Wait!' he shouted, 'Wait!' He thought, we could be killed up here, and nobody would know. It was strange how when one loved somebody, fear could spurt suddenly out of happiness; he felt the spurt when he saw her run and trip.

'Oh, James!' He saw her half-turn, heard her cry out to him, saw her stand stockstill, staring down at the ground. Past a little hide made for birdwatchers, past a mound of blackened gorse sticks left from a fire, past a stone cairn that marked the way up he ran, caught her up, stood beside her and saw what she saw. The bare stony ground covered with yellow flowers that seemed to glow like pale gold; it was impossible that they had grown there; they must have been put there, stuck in, a minute before. And that exuberance, that gratitude moved in him again: they had seen the flowers that would only bloom for an hour, that while one looked away would wither and die. And he himself was strong and yet vulnerable, he would plod ahead of her or behind up that mountain to the very top, now he would never tire; yet one look from her, as she scampered about and found shells and stones and flowers for him would undo him. The rocks, the peaks strengthened him; it was liquid light in the valley, the ready-to-vanish flowers, that look of hers, sideways, that he could never quite seize, that made him weak. He saw now that the hidden strength in her that he had hunted for in his mind and not been able to find, was after all a familiar one. It was not aggressive or ambition or a desire to conquer heights that had made her want to climb the mountain; it was simply the curiosity that made her run from rock to tree, collecting things; which when satisfied made her seem sometimes petulant. She wanted to know what it was like, as she wanted to know what that shell was like, and how long ago the sea might have left it there. Once she had examined the shell, she had no more use for it, she threw it down on the path, ignorant of keepsake or nostalgia; it was he who picked it up to put in his shirt pocket. There would be the moment when they reached the top, he knew now, when he would have to stand and savour it, making himself empty to receive impressions, when she, having seen what it was like, grew instantly bored and wanted to go down. This was a fact of their life now. Having observed this, he found himself instantly more mature, protective. On the day on which she paused, began to reflect, he would be there to receive her. He would still have the shell, probably, and she might recognise at last the feeling that had prompted him to pick it up, all those years ago.

On they went, and the bushes grew sparser, the rocks smaller and more easily dislodged, as they passed on a zigzag track under the great shoulder of rock that began the peak. The earth was red between the stones; and there was a patch of dried horse droppings; and then they were on a windy bare surface where no horse could have gone and little earth grew, where there were only small succulents sprouting, as in a desert, where the wind cleaned all loose and fragile things away. There would be a climb, now, a real climb up a rockface. James looked for a moment at Charlotte, to see if this was what she really wanted; but he did not ask, her face was set, it was up to him to lead the way. It seemed to be at this moment that they became aware of ribbed cloud drawn like a veil across the sun, and felt the cold of season as well as altitude touch them. As the sky grew cloudier, the outline of rock became less clear, it was not so easy to plan a way, foresee a foothold, as it had been. For it had been the stripe of deep shadow that had showed the cleft in the rock and the hollowed path; now all the surface seemed smoother and less accessible.

Charlotte said, at his frown, 'It's only a cloud, only one cloud. God, doesn't being out of England make one a perfectionist?' But the cloud, thin, almost imperceptible, spread as if pulled out at the edges, to filter the sun.

'All right? Shall I go on up?' He saw her nod, a slight crease of effort between her eyebrows as she stretched to grasp a rock and bring herself up beside him. He was methodical in his climbing; never move a hand or foot unless you have safe holds for the other three. And he went on, not fast but surely, stretching, gripping, finding another hole. The toes of his boots found support in the smallest crevices, his hands grew stronger, tested surfaces, rejected loose stones, felt about for a sure handhold. It seemed to have a mechanical ease, this climb; as if the rock had waited all this time for him, its contours the perfect foil to his own. His mind blank, he felt only a physical satisfaction as he climbed, an exhilaration in the actual movement, the actual contact of flesh to rock. Tiny plants flourished at eye level, their roots drawing nourishment from a few grains of sandy earth. Above him a single dead tree jutted, relic of the time when all Provence had been forested, the mountains themselves hidden in pine. There had been fires here, even this high up; he saw the stains on stones and an occasional twig like charcoal. If he bent his head back a little now, he saw the final ledge over which they must haul themselves, before the less difficult ascent to the final peak. Up there were bushes again, sprouting against the widely patterned sky. It would be possible to stand upright there, the real climb would be over. His hand gripped the edge of the final boulder of its own accord, he felt a tiny shower of pebbles fall from beneath his right boot. It had not occurred to him to pause, look down, or think of going back. Only now, as the pebbles falling scattered far down the rock, did he think of Charlotte.

'Are you all right?' he called back, his voice muffled even to himself as his mouth was so close to the rockface.

'Yes.' There was no tone in her voice, nothing to warn him. Reassured, he swung himself up the last bit, over the whitened smooth piece of rock spattered with bird droppings with a scramble on to his knees and a grip at the wiry prickly bush that grew only just in reach. He sat, legs dangling, and felt a tingling that began in his scratched, torn fingers begin to spread through his whole body; he panted and smiled at the sky and felt the blood pounding in his ears; he had extended himself, he was fully alive. Then he saw Charlotte's white face at the level of his feet and the mood of easy triumph sprang away. He was on his knees, leaning over, he stretched a hand to her, and noticing to his surprise that it was bleeding, he said, 'Here, take my hand, I'll pull you up.' Her whole weight was suspended from his hand for a moment and he was unprepared for her total dependence; he saw her feet feel about ineffectually for a hold, then her knees come up on the ledge and her body collapse at the side of his where he fell back upon the prickly bush. They lay there, side by side upon the ledge, and felt the wind tearing over them. There was the sky, now almost entirely covered by the rib-pattern of cloud, a pinkish tinge where the sun had been. And there was silence, apart from their breathing; not even a stone moved.

James said quietly, 'Are you all right?'

She propped herself on an elbow, looked down at him. Her colour, in those few minutes, had quite returned, she was rosy and tanned as he knew her well. 'Phew,' she said, 'That was quite a climb, wasn't it? And we aren't even at the top yet. Still, the next bit looks easy enough.'

'D'you want to go on?'

'Of course I do. Don't you? Look, it's hardly any way now.' Cloud surrounded the mountain top now, puffy cloud from inland having come to join the fishbone cloud from the sea.

'It's a pity about the weather,' Charlotte said. James fingered the white shell in his pocket; but was not sure, even these moments afterwards of the memory of the face of fear that had appeared between his feet. They stood, and went on hand in hand, their hands hanging rather limply between them. Suddenly there was once again a zigzag path to follow, the white stone clear between dark scrub. The path widened, became once again an outcrop. There was a last scramble, easy after the climb, and they were at the top of the mountain.

It was only a moment, there was only time to draw breath, before they heard voices. It was not possible; they glanced at each other, signalling their disbelief.

'Yes,' James said, 'Listen. You're right. There are.' And a man and a woman appeared from behind a rock on the other side of the little plateau, and came towards them. They lifted hands in greeting, as if they had been in a street. A first impression was of white teeth and gold, brown faces; the woman's eyes as blue as Charlotte's but surrounded by tiny lines.

'Bonjour,' the man said — middle-aged, strong-looking, grey-haired and brown as stained wood — and held out a hand, palm up.

'Bonjour,' said James, startled into formality, and took the hand offered. The woman smiled at Charlotte, raising an eyebrow to mock the men's conventionality. 'I'm sorry, she said in French, 'That we were here already, to spoil your mountain top for you.'

Charlotte said, 'Well, I'm sorry to have disturbed you. After all, you got here first.' She was easy, conversational, colloquial. James simply smiled at the man whose hand he had gripped, and fell back a pace, to establish a gap between them. He thought, I can't possibly remember any French up here.

'Which way did you come up?' the man asked, looking puzzled, 'Because we've only just come, I'm surprised that we didn't meet you.' James pointed straight down and said, 'Nous avons grimpe.' The man's mouth pursed, he had not understood. Charlotte explained, 'We came up through the little pine wood at the bottom, from the village, and then a long way up a track, and then up a sort of precipice on to that ledge down there, and then on a little path again. Which way did you come?'

'Tiens,' the man turned to his wife, waving his hands, 'They came straight up, like mountain goats! Why did you come straight up the rock? There's a track that comes all the way up, didn't you know? What would old people like us do otherwise? Good God, you picked a dangerous way up.'

James tried to say, 'We didn't know there was another way,' and foundered.

The older man said, admiringly, 'She must be strong, your wife. This is your wife? Excuse me,

I didn't introduce us. My name is Maurice Coudonnet, and this is my wife. Francoise, did you hear that, they came straight up the rockface.' He repeated it to her, pointing with his forefinger straight up in the air; but she said smoothly, 'Well, it's possible to do these things when you are young. We are grandparents, you know, we used to be more adventurous once, but not any more.'

At once, Charlotte began to ask eagerly about the grandchildren, the children, where they lived, what they did. And charmed by her real interest, the older woman, with a light rise and fall of her hands as she spoke, began to tell her. 'My daughter lives in Paris now, yes, they were all born in the Midi, I am from Marseille, and we will have our little granddaughter to stay next week, my daughter and her husband are going to Germany —'

James said, across the feet of stone that separated him from the husband, 'I'm sorry, I don't speak French well. My wife —'

'Ah,' the man interrupted, 'I understand you quite well. You must have confidence. Confidence, that is all. Speak, and you will be understood. You must not be embarrassed.

After all, where are we? On the top of a mountain.'

And James laughed, acknowledging the absurdity, as the cold wind blew around the four of them, flapping their clothes against them, flattening their hair across their faces; and moved a step nearer to listen. The man's face was endlessly mobile, his eyebrows went up and down, his lips drew back fastidiously to emit vowel sounds, showing the twin gold teeth behind his canines, even his nose moved and his grey scalp shifted on his skull. His hands, broad brown climber's hands, drew outlines against the sky. And his eyes, grey, deepset, looked into James' own with a deliberate curiosity. 'Who are you?' his eyes were saying, 'Why have I met you here?' While he talked of the war, of having been with the Free French, of having been briefly in London where he had learned a few phrases of forgotten English; of Churchill, of Europe, of the world in which he now found himself growing old. 'The important thing is to use your life,' he said, 'Never believe that you will have another one. This is all,' and his hands took in the far mountains, the valley, the tiny farmhouses thousands of feet below. 'It's enough, isn't it?' he said, and his smile of irony broadened into a grin. 'That is why we come up here, my wife and I. Oh, in the old days we used to do some real climbing. But she is fifty-five now, my wife. I am sixty soon. For a man, that is not so old. Women have less stamina, perhaps, less strength. But one must not under-estimate their spirit. For pure spirit, my wife would fly up a mountain. It is I who have to remind her that she is no longer young. But we have a good life, still, oh yes.'

James, understanding what he said although he spoke in the rolling accent of southern France, nodded and leaned forward and opened his mouth every now and then to agree.

'How long have you been married?'

'A year.' He looked across at Charlotte, who stood next to Madame Coudonnet, talking animatedly to her, a lock of black hair falling across her face to be brushed back with an impatient hand. He could not hear what they were saying; he saw the older woman's grave attention break suddenly into laughter, he saw how Charlotte held and then released that attention, making the other person relax. There was something in her stance that was so familiar — from parties in London, from the time when he had first known her — that a hand seemed to close suddenly around his heart. He drew breath, knew the older man's glance upon him. They stood there, the two of them, without speaking, and their attention turned upon Charlotte. She, noticing it, broke off what she was saying to glance back, smile, acknowledge them, and then continue her anecdote. The older woman, tolerant, smiled round too. James saw for a moment upon Maurice Coudonnet's face an expression — warm, musing, concerned — that startled him. He was looking at Charlotte; Charlotte chatting and laughing upon a mountain top as if she had been in a drawing room, but with her black hair whipped about her pink cheeks. James intercepted the look and was all at once wary. But M. Coudonnet had taken him into consideration too. 'Look after her,' he said, 'Won't you?' And James simply said, 'Of course.'

There seemed to be no convention established for leaving a mountain top, no way of saying goodbye. They all glanced at each other, mocking themselves, wondering who would move first. It was like that time at a party, James thought, after one has said goodbye, after one has thanked everybody; when for some reason one is still there in the hall, still talking but carrying one's coat. He knew that Charlotte hated such prolonged farewells; he also knew that she unfairly expected him to move first.

'Well,' he said now, 'We'd better be going down now, I think,' and to his surprise the French phrases seemed to fall quite elegantly into place, 'Our bus leaves at five. It was nice meeting you. Thank you for letting us share your mountain top. Goodbye, Madame, goodbye, Monsieur.' They all shook hands with great affection; ease was re-established after the momentary doubt. The older couple, like parents, waved and smiled as James and Charlotte began their descent. 'No precipices on the way down, now,' Maurice Coudonnet called gaily down to them; and James and Charlotte turned and waved, more lighthearted than they had been all day, and shouted back, certainly not.

'What nice people,' James said, taking her hand, guiding her into the zigzag path; they skipped carelessly down, making small avalanches of stones where they had come so laboriously up. It was easy, to have been up and to go down.

Charlotte said, 'I suppose if one climbs a mountain there is bound to be somebody interesting at the top. I mean, they would hardly be boring.' The thought reverberated in his mind as they strode with tired legs back into the village, in the narrow lane hung with jasmine and wisteria where the walls warmed them with preserved heat and the flowers seemed to have retained the light of early morning throughout the greyness of afternoon. He thought of the people she would be bound to meet on desert islands and remote shores; and of how he would suddenly, in some strange language, once again find his tongue. Forgetting for the moment the rock climb, as he had during the climb forgotten her, he felt himself follow her willingly into a populated, communicative, optimistic world.

Dans le train

Imagine it. An express train going south through the night towards dawn. A closed train that stops only once, two o'clock in the morning, at an arbitrary point. Remember the claustrophobia of couchettes? The door is pulled to and clicks shut, the plastic blinds are down. Above or below, strangers stacked upon shelves, their unfamiliar night sounds, a groan in dream, a waking cough. The smell of feet, plastic bottles, rough blankets. Skin sticks to the hard bed where the slip of sheet has come away. You turn on to your back, the surface above you only inches from your nose. You cannot sit up, but turn on your elbow, fiddle in a coat pocket to find a watch, stare at the luminous dial, feel for the sharp outline of a wrapped aspirin tablet, bring out a wet rank flannel from a polythene bag to wipe your forehead cool. There is a strip, beneath the blind on the window, that shows yellow when lights pass, that flickers occasionally with outside movement; that is the strip where dawn will show, a grey line at long last. Enough. Imagine the relief of sleep after a long day, after experiencing all this, even though the experience has only lasted for ten minutes. Sleep. You are carried through the darkness of an unknown countryside at eighty miles an hour or more; you sleep; above and below you they sleep; from outside the train is blind, shuttered, thirty carriages locked against intrusion. The image is one of inevitability. Now that you are on the train, that is it, you are locked up and carried along. Imagine.

To imagine something fully is to make it inevitable. You think of saying something, the words form in your head; and it is out, in public. 'I wish you would go away and leave me alone!' Suppress it, and it is still there, one day it will pop out on its own. I imagine that something might happen on this train. A train is a good place for a writer to imagine, as snowed-up houses have been, and ships crossing the

Atlantic. I do not know what it will be, yet. The story is on the train, carried along in the night; it is wrapped and labelled in the luggage van, it is between people in the restaurant as the waiter comes, spilling soup on the plates' rims, it is in one of those closed carriages where people already turn to sleep. You will spot the allegory. But this tidiness, this inevitability, this neat fit of image to actuality, symbol to thought, how am I to break it, how show you the roughness, the inconclusiveness of what happened? How say, this was real; this, because it is past, has been made up?

Imagine. Fiction is an attack in the night, an unpredictable assault that will not justify itself. To you, it does not often happen. You are a woman in a train, sitting down to eat dinner as the train leaves the channel port, unfolding a large fresh napkin, looking up with anticipation for the first course. Or you are a man, staring out into the dusk as yellow lights turn in a farmyard outside, cows move white patches of flank, a village is past, a forest, a field. A man and a woman together, that is it; who have made many such journeys together yet who recently have hardly had time to be alone; who are relishing the gaps between words, the long pauses between actions; for whom the sealed train provides an image of renewed, sustained privacy. You think, pleasure increases, grows upon itself. There is more pleasure in travelling through darkening northern France, eating dinner, than once there was; because you have kept an image in your mind, of what it is like, or what it might be like. Because of your expectations there is more of France, more of the darkening evening. It is there in your mind, it has simply to unfurl, and more again will be added to it. That tree was there already, that low Norman farm was expected, and the youths in the little square shouting around a battered Citroen, pointing their arms. That bird perched upon a wire is new, the horse galloping is new, the way he stops at the fence and throws up his head, a mere gleam in twilight; the moon rising has never had quite that colour. Amiens. The empty station platforms, the large blue hanging sign; associations of a name. Some thoughts are inevitable, one cannot help thinking them. But the quiche is here, and the half bottle of wine for each of you. The child opposite is staring and pushing bread into her mouth. The door clangs open and the men are poised above the tables, expertly handing plates.

So, after this meal you are bound to sleep well, even in the confines of your couchettes. You walk back the long way up the train, bumping into walls as the train sways and rocks and picks up speed, flattening yourself to let people pass, passing flattened others with a word, 'Pardon ...' And there you are, the place is recognisable because of the pale sandy-haired young man who is lounging against the window outside your compartment. The one you saw earlier, putting his child to bed, tenderly undressing the tired two-year-old who is asleep now in the bottom bunk, her mother's arm curled around her. He is alone, family man, responsible father, young in spite of it, abrupt in his movements as you approach. The holiday? It was my wife's idea. She would bring the kid camping. She's crazy that way. You listen, half concentrating, looking out into the darkness, agreeing, thinking of tired children carried across Europe, of nappies and bottles of congealing milk. The heat grows, between the close walls, there is only a slight draught from the window. The young Australian from the next compartment passes with a full bottle of whisky; he is naked to the waist, gently tanned, with pink nipples and a girl's mouth, his hair down his back. He passes the bottle, is surprised at your refusal, at the sandy young man's. You go to bed now, lying down partly dressed, accepting the cramped place; expecting nothing but morning, imagining nothing but a new day.

You might imagine that you are a writer wakened in the night by shouts, thuds, breaking glass, a scream. Or equally, that you are a doctor on holiday with your husband, taking a needed rest, wakened by the same sounds, opening a compartment door upon blood and confusion, finding a surgical case waiting upon your doorstep. Which of them is ministering to the other's need for interruption; for accidents, for happenings? What about the other people there, woken in the night? You are one of the other people there, who has not imagined anything. Is it fair? Fiction is an assault in the night. Imagining nothing, you wake slowly, tiredly, wondering what all this noise is. Paris is past, there you were dimly aware of shunting, bumping, people moving about; and of noise from the next compartment where the Australian and Tanzanian boys are, shouts and song and laughter and crashes. After Paris you slept again, so that now you are waking in the middle of nowhere, an uncharted time and place, in the country, in the night. The compartment door is open, light from the corridor makes you blink.

Des, Des; oh, don't let him; please, don't, keep still, keep still. A girl's voice pleads, she is leaning from the lower bunk, protecting with her body the sleeping child. Outside, a scuffling in the passage, buffeting at the door, voices. Keep still. Keep still and do as you're told. You've got quite a bad head wound, do you know that? Don't be a damn fool. Keep still. Has anybody got any cotton wool?

You have cotton wool, you fumble for it, pass it. It is your first action.

Has anybody got a scarf?

You have a scarf.

I'm going to have to stitch this. When you get off the train, you'll have to get him to a hospital. Can you do that?

Yes, yes. The girl speaks distractedly.

And the blurred, shouting voice you will come to know so well says over and over; just let me get at the ones that did it. I'll kill them, just let me get at them, the bastards, where are they, I'll kill —

There is something in this scene that is entirely unacceptable to you; you close your eyes and assume that in a minute it will all be over, quick as a dream. But no. You are not the lady doctor in the long dress and cloak who is there because she is a doctor, who has to be involved. You are not the girl in the bottom bunk with the sleeping child, who has seen all this before, who perhaps knows what happens next. But you are there, shut in, close to it all. You will not get away, not without having to understand. You are the innocent bystander. What will you do?

He is uncontrollable, he is bellowing in the corridor, shouting for his wife, for the child, shouting obscenities, standing with a shoe raised and the heel pointed, for anyone who will stand between him and his wife. The lady doctor, having mopped and bandaged, has gone back to bed. What else can she do? He tears off your flimsy scarf and the cotton wool, he stands there bleeding and threatening, whisky-drunk. You have never before seen anybody who is beyond the reach of reason. You speak to him: leave her alone! Your voice shakes, and he shouts it all again, for you this time, shit and cunt and fuck and sodding whore.

Ça, alors. The Frenchwoman who is travelling with her seven-year-old daughter in the same compartment, whose shoe it is, whose hair he has already pulled, begins to mutter to herself in French and drag her sleepy daughter from her bed to find a place somewhere else. The little girl, sitting up in her vest, her dark hair ruffled and black eyes big with sleep and surprise, watches it all. And her mother slips her down and they take a single bag and move away, out of sight; there are other spaces further down the train; a girl in the corridor sympathetically helps them along. You are left. You cannot get down from your bunk and move elsewhere, because of the woman, younger than you, who cries out, don't let him get me, don't. Of course not, you say, and, don't be afraid. He pushes the door wide open and barges in once the Frenchwoman and her child are gone. You are aware of people standing behind him in the corridor, people anxious to help, not knowing what to do, talking in English and French, asking each other questions; what happened, what is happening; he should be stopped; oui, mais il est fort comme un boeuf; he is bleeding still; he says they hit him with a bottle; oh, it's always happening, his wife says, trying again, get into bed, Des, and what about Polly, little Polly, look, she needs you; forget about me, it's all right for me, but look at her, look at Polly.

Fuck her, she's irrelevant.

You, listening, feel your wrists swollen with anger, your hands tremble. The man opposite you, with whom you have lived for years, tries now to get the other into the corridor, to shut him out. The fighting voice with the blurred sound, familiar now, shouts, I'll kill you. The two men are in the corridor, suddenly it seems that everybody else has dispersed. The night is like this, the audience comes and goes.

I'll kill you. This is the last you hear. Quick, shut the door. The door is shut, darkness entire; the lights do not work in here. Time hangs in suspension, there are sounds, thuds from outside, as if a heavy parcel is beaten to and fro from wall to wall. I'll kill you, he said; fort comme un boeuf, armed with a high-heeled shoe. Quick, shut the door. His wife says, don't let him, don't. The child Polly wakes and turns and is about to cry. You say, give me the child; the limp, heavy, warm familiarity of her. You take her up to the top bunk with you, hold her with her teddy, smooth her nightdress down over round white knees. Her mother crouches on the other top bunk. She says, I'm sorry, I'm so sorry. Time elapses, not very much perhaps, and the man you live with slips back, quick as a flash, round the door, and shuts it behind him; all the buttons are torn off his shirt and his hand is bitten. He climbs to the top bunk beside the young woman whose hair falls in a brown cascade, who begins to tell you how it has all happened. The siege begins, the prolonged angry battering of the door from outside.

Fuck you, open the door, my wife and child —

He has done this before. Never so bad as this, but this sort of thing —

My wife and child are in there, Christ almighty, open the bloody —

The trouble is, I'm a coward. I can't stand it. I've left him twice —

Crash. Crash. I'll break the bloody door down —

But he would come, he wouldn't let me take Polly camping on my own, I should have known —

Crash. Crash. Sod. Fuck. I'll get you, you bleeding whore —

I'm sorry you had to get involved —

Crash. Crash.

Not at all. Don't worry. It must be ghastly for you. What a nice teddy you have Polly, what a nice —

Mummy, is Daddy naughty, Mummy, what is Daddy doing?

Nothing darling, Daddy'll be all right in the morning, there's a good girl. In a minute you will see the door beginning to give. You are all crouched high up like frightened monkeys on perches, watching the strain of the door. Melodrama has taken over. What do you do?

Pull the communication cord. It is stiff, you have to pull a communication cord extremely hard and then it sags away in your hand, there is a long hiss, as of escaping gas; for a moment you entertain the fantasy that you will be gassed, there on your bunk. And after a long moment of doubt, it happens; the whole great train stops in the middle of nowhere. It is a long time before anything happens at all, but you have the feeling that time may be lasting longer than it should. At first, the sound of footsteps on the track outside makes you think that he has come round this way, to get into the compartment by smashing the window. But there are voices in the corridor, once the brake has been released. Again, it is a long time before you understand that they are asking you to open the door, that it is safe to do so. When you open it, you look out with the mad stare of a prisoner too long in the dark, waiting for the next attack.

Who pulled the communication cord?

You did. After reading about penalties for improper use.

Forty francs, please. That is the first lesson of French justice, that it does not pay to be the victim.

Mais, monsieur, cet homme nous a terrorise.

Forty francs.

I'll pay, no, no, we will, no, really, honestly, here's the money, no, please, this is his money, he can pay for it himself.

You see it folded and pocketed and a notebook produced. Sa femme. Son adresse. Son passe-port. He can be put off the train at Dijon, handed over to the police.

Only if she comes too. That is the second lesson, that you cannot escape from your attacker, if you are married to him, carry his name. You go with him, like a certificate.

A girl has appeared from somewhere, red-haired, efficient, completely bilingual and is translating. It is a play in two languages. He says, elle dit, elle ne parle pas français. He says you have to go with him, that as his wife you are legally responsible for him, if he is not responsible for his own actions. Oui, madame. You all protest; she says she will not go.

A young man, southern French in blue denim, a piece of horn on a silver chain around his neck, interrupts vehemently from the corridor, you must not give him over to the police, not that, you do not know what you would be doing, you must keep him on the train. Everybody is strangely subdued by him, his is the voice of authority.

The girl with the flushed face and falling brown hair, who does not speak French, who knows what always must happen next, says that he may stay on the train as long as he is locked up for the night.

You begin to believe that there will be an end. You are suddenly exhausted, you think of nothing but sleep. Nobody has been killed, but violence has moved in with you for part of a night, filled the place in which you are enclosed. That is all. Imagine it.

In the morning, the first word you hear is 'Avignon'. The sound fuses with the strip of greenish light that lies along the bottom of the blind when you open your eyes, a different quality of light from any you have seen for so long; strong southern sunlight. Out in the corridor people stand and lean upon their elbows, watch the empty early morning stations pass and the wild rocky countryside in between, watch the light spread and strengthen, the sky deepen, there is a delicacy of colour, an exactness of shadow. Inside the train everybody comes to look longingly out, waiting to be released. And you recognise faces from the drama of the night, but it is like seeing actors off stage resting after an arduous part. The vehement young man, an anarchist perhaps, his bilingual girl-friend with red hair, the doctor in her long dress, her husband, the Frenchwoman from Marseille and her daughter, the half-naked Australian, his Tanzanian friend. Their faces are drained of colour, their bodies of movement; and now that they have nearly arrived, they are strangers to each other and to you. The girl with the two-year-old on the bottom bunk lifts her child on to her knee and begins to brush her hair. The child looks up at you and does not recognise you; the mother speaks to nobody, as if there is no point. Out in the corridor a young man appears; his face is unfamiliar, hair sandy, skin paper-white, eyes veined with red; only when he speaks are you sure. The northern English voice, flat vowels, clipped urban consonants. He bends to help his wife dress the child, they begin to unload their camping gear on to the floor, to pack away the baby's food and their own hairbrushes and magazines into a basket, you would say that this was any young couple setting out on a camping holiday with their child. He looks up, his apology comes out as an accusation; you are making me sorry for something I know nothing about. There is no answer; such an apology is irrelevant; the man you live with, whose shirt still gapes buttonless, tells him. The young man is lost now, he is the actor stripped of a role, who has nothing else to do but act; he is lost and closed to himself until the next time. You cannot see him without cold dislike. And his wife; what you see, what shocks you, is her docility. I've left him twice. The trouble is, I'm a coward, you see. He has done this before. What shocks you is that nothing is unforgiveable. The night is over, morning has come. Like travelling players they pack their things and pick up their child and move on towards the next situation. Another time, another place, and others will be used as adjuncts to their story; others, not you, will be assaulted out of sleep in the night.

Avignon, Arles, Tarascon, Marseille. The rocky country, the red earth, the industrial basins, rising chimneys, further mountains, blue blurred Mediterranean sea. Now I will let you free. There is a crisp wind blowing, and even at the Gare St. Charles the air fills your lungs with relief. The great grey metal train waits, and the people get out, tired, unwashed, carrying their possessions lopsidedly. You are among them. You are about to become anonymous, a tourist as you wanted to be, ordering breakfast, strolling in the sunshine down to the old port, looking at boats, looking at people; sitting under the plane trees undisturbed. For you do not want to be disturbed. It is your only positive thought, I do not ever have to see them again. Coincidence, other meetings, the inextricable involvement of one life with another, these are the tricks of fiction, they need not concern you now. Sitting at a cafe, while hot coffee is brought, and croissants, while the man in the green apron moves about on the still wet floor, you begin to talk about it all, to see if it is possible in this raw moment afterwards to tell how it really was. But no, he moved first, I was outside, it was after that that we —

You are free now, though, you may tell it how you like. They are all gone, the drunkard, the wife, the lady doctor, the anarchist, the official, the red-head, the Frenchwoman, the Australian, all dispersed. The story is yours to tell.

www.ingramcontent.com/pod-product-compliance
Lightning Source LLC
Chambersburg PA
CBHW020053180626
46812CB00006B/2317